THE ZOMBIE WARS
THE ENEMY WITHIN

JOSEPH TALLUTO

SEVERED PRESS
HOBART TASMANIA

THE ZOMBIE WARS

WWW.SEVEREDPRESS.COM

ISBN: 978-1-925342-51-2

IOWA

"How many?"

"We don't have to talk about this now."

"I hate repeating myself."

"Forty-three."

"Mother of God."

"Not your fault, sir."

"Yes, it is. I sent them in, and they died."

"Had to be done, sir."

"I know. And I'd do it again, God help me."

I stayed out of the conversation since this was Charlie's command. We had been on the road for just a few weeks now making our way across the state of Illinois and into Iowa. At Sarah's insistence, we had waited until the first hard frost had arrived, and then we had set out. We had been on the road for seven months prior and had managed to clear out a huge swath of the United States of the majority of zombies. We couldn't get them all, but we had managed to get enough of them that they weren't a constant danger. The cities we had left alone. Hundreds of thousands of zombies, possibly millions, was just something we weren't able to deal with. So we used the highways that ringed most major metropolitan areas and turned them into barricades. Chicago was the exception. That one we used cargo containers to keep it locked up, and if I had to do it all over again, I'd have opted for the highway method. We took the biggest earthmovers we could find and basically tore up the asphalt, piling it on the city side. Bulldozers followed, creating trenches that would contain an outbreak if the zombies found a way over. It was crude but effective.

I snapped out of my musings when Charlie repeated my name. "John?"

"I'm sorry, drifted away there for a moment. What was the question?" I asked, looking from Charlie to the soldier who was waiting by the door.

"Will you say something at the burial?" Charlie asked.

"Of course. Be glad to. Sorry," I said.

Charlie dismissed the soldier with a quick salute. Then he turned to me.

"Where's your head?" he asked. "Don't tell me it's with Sarah and your boys."

I pointed to the map on the wall of the trailer we were using as a command center. "That's a lot of country to cover, brother," I said. "Starting to have some doubts about this."

Charlie nodded. "I hear you. But we're in this to finish it. I don't want my daughter or your sons having to worry about getting attacked when they take a stroll down the road. Nor anyone else's kids for that matter."

"There is that. I was thinking about splitting the army again," I said, pointing to the northern states. "These states weren't heavily populated even when there weren't any zombies around. If we send maybe three thousand to sweep north," I said, moving my hand across Minnesota, North Dakota, and Montana, "we can clear three states and see if our neighbors to the north had managed to weather the storm as well."

Charlie nodded. "Makes sense. With the numbers we have now, we can split again like we did before and cover more ground."

"No going off on our own again, though," I said.

"Hell, no. That was enough for me." Charlie shook his head. "Rebecca was a wreck and was not happy about all the things I told her."

"Why do you tell everything, anyway?" I asked. "She just gets more worried every time you step out the door."

"Don't ever want to go to my maker knowing I lied to my wife before I had a chance to apologize," Charlie said simply.

"Fair enough. Now let's go over this mess we got ourselves into right now. Forty-three dead? That was a hell of a fight," I said.

Charlie pointed to the map of the town in front of him. "We did everything we did before. Run through with a vehicle, walk through opening doors, draw them out, and kill them. Pretty straight forward. Worked a dozen times before."

"But…"

"But this time they stayed hidden until we came in strength, and they hit us from the rear. Ten people were down in the first wave of the attack. Four people died from friendly fire, and the rest just got isolated and overwhelmed," Charlie said, shaking his head. "I should have seen it. They've been getting smarter, and I didn't see it."

It was my turn to shake my head. "How could you possibly have known? If anything, I should have set up a research lab at the capitol to study the Z's and see how they were progressing in their evolution. No one could have known," I said. "But if there is any benefit to this, we know now. And what we will do is set up a second line that walks through behind the first, and if the zombies come out to play, they'll find themselves between two really pissed off groups of survivors."

Charlie nodded. "Good. Good. We'll tell the fighters that. They'll like the trap."

"Settles that problem then. When is the burial?" I asked, looking out the window.

"I dunno. Figured we'd get it down tomorrow, and be done with it. No point in waiting, and the ground is getting harder to dig through." Charlie said.

"All right. Come get me before hand, and I'll do the service," I said.

"You okay? You seem someplace else," Charlie asked with a slight tilt of his head.

I nodded. "Just thinking about the whole situation. I'm all right," I said, clapping Charlie on the shoulder.

I left the small command office and walked through the camp. We were in Iowa, and contrary to what most people thought, Iowa wasn't just flatlands and farmland. On the eastern end, anyway, there were rolling hills, deep streams, and about a thousand places for zombies to hide.

We kept the camp mobile, using vans and RV's and trucks to transport everyone. When we travelled, we tended to split into four or five groups, pick a destination, and clear all of the zombies out of the area we could find before the rendezvous. We took what was useful from unoccupied homes and left alone anyone who was still alive. Most of the time we gave them supplies as they needed them. We cleared out every small town and home of any zombies leaving them ready for anyone to come and reclaim. Sarah and Rebecca had put a lot of thought into this, and we agreed that it would be best not to try and get everyone to come back to the capital, but to leave them where they were comfortable, and ninety-nine percent zombie free.

As the Chief Executive, I was given a huge RV for the war, but I downsized it to something a little easier to maneuver through the back roads of America. I gave the RV to a platoon of women to use as their home while I hooked up a travel trailer to a Ford F150 king cab. I preferred the idea of being able to bug out with the truck and not have to try and manage a bus. As far as the platoon was concerned, any group of zombies dumb enough to tackle them was going to have a very short time to regret it before their undead life became their very dead life.

The chill air was welcome for a very short time, and then I was hunching my shoulders against it. I pulled my hood up and watched as the November winds played out across the prairie. Old crops swayed with the breezes, and here and there was a rustle of movement as a rodent of some sort made a sortie out for food.

I walked to the top of a small hill, and it gave me a slight vantage point for looking over the camp. We were several miles out of Cedar Rapids, and I had sent scouts ahead to see if there was any easy way to deal with the threat. The cold weather worked to our advantage, slowing down the zombies, but they were evolving ever so slightly, and they knew enough to try and stay out of the cold if they could help it. Bad news for them, they could never stay inside when food was nearby. Bad news for us, they could never stay inside when we were nearby. But they were sluggish enough that our best defense was a quick walk out of danger. I planned to use the cold to our advantage and clean up as many as we could without taking too many casualties. Charlie's raid blew that apart, but I wasn't going to fault him for it. Who knew an entire middle school had turned, and the pre-teens were going to attack from the rear? As it was, had it been summer and they were as fast as they could have been, they'd have wiped out that entire command.

The RV's, trucks, and trailers lined the road, and we stayed in contact through CB radios and hand held radios. Everyone was required to turn on their radio at eight o'clock at night for the next day's instructions. I could see the flickering lights of lamps and candles as I walked past, and I returned the salute of several fighters as they returned from patrol.

When I started this fight, I figured to lead the grand army to victory. But I learned I was better at small unit tactics and wound up off on my own. I then realized I didn't like letting other people go off and fight for me when I wasn't with them. I decided to put the army back together, but lead it like it was a small unit. So far, it worked like a charm. Then we got ambushed. Have to settle that tomorrow.

"Sir!"

I turned at the voice and found myself looking at a young man, likely no older than eighteen. He was dressed warmly, with his weapons strapped on the outside his coat. His forearms were covered in sheet metal ductwork, a trick the deep scouts used to gain a second if they found themselves in a bad situation. His dark eyes were serious, and he had seen more in his young life than many people before him had seen in several lifetimes.

I recognized him after a minute. "Hassad, right?" I asked, shifting out of the wind.

"Yes, sir. Thank you, sir. I went to Commander James, and he said to find you. The scout of Cedar Rapids is finished," Hassad said.

"And?" I asked.

"Original population was around a hundred thousand, sir. We counted at least half that, probably more."

I thought about it. "Good enough. We'll go over the rest of the report in the morning. And Hassad?"

"Sir?"

"Shoot that zombie up there, would you?" I asked, pointing to the slow moving figure that had appeared about five hundred yards away. It moved with the unmistakable shamble of a ghoul, and it was headed right for camp.

Hassad slipped his rifle off his shoulder and aimed for a second. I could see him adjusting his aim for the wind, and then he let the shot go. I watched for a second, and then the zombie shifted to the side, falling down.

Hassad shouldered his rifle and smiled at me.

"Anything else, sir?" he asked.

I smiled back. Several heads poked out of doors, watching us, and looking out their windows to see if they could see what he was shooting at.

"He's getting up, Hassad."

"Shit! Not for long." The young man took off across the land, making a straight line for the zombie. When he reached a closer hill, he stopped, aimed for a longer moment, and then made a killing shot. Truth be known, I would have been stunned had he made a killing shot at five hundred yards. Just hitting a zombie at that distance was hard, and he had done it in a good wind. I smiled when I figured he'd be harder on himself than I could ever be with him. It was times like this that I thought about my friend Nate and how much we could use his experience and knowledge in this fight.

I reached my trailer and stopped for a moment. Around us, the long grasses swayed in the evening breeze. It was cold but not bad, especially for the Midwest. I had lived here for years, so I knew what the storms could be like, but I also knew that we had long stretches of cold without snow that would serve us very well right now. Keep the zombies slow but make sure we could see them. Snow covered Z's were not fun when spring came and thawed them out.

A young hawk soared overhead, likely looking for a place to spend the night. We had a lot of them following us. Our passage usually spooked the game in the area making hunting easier. If we were a flotilla, I guess they'd be sharks.

"Daddy!" Jake's voice was the first thing I heard when I entered the trailer. He was playing at the table while Sarah was feeding Aaron. Aaron was a big boy, likely to become a big man. Sarah looked up briefly then went back to feeding. Jake came off the seat with a bounce and jumped into my arms.

"When we leave, Daddy?" Jake asked, pulling at my coat. "Will we leave soon? Soon?"

I tussled his hair and looked into his deep brown eyes. "When we finish here, buddy. We've got a lot of work to do tomorrow."

"Can I see a cow? Are there cows around here? When can I see a cow?" Jake barely stopped for a breath, his eyes already looking out the windows for a cow we couldn't see if it was in front of us.

"Soon, pal, soon. Can Daddy take off his gear and settle in before you ask too many questions?" I said, putting him back onto the floor.

"Can I have a snack?" Jake asked, turning his big brown eyes on me.

"Ahem!" Sarah looked up again and gave Jake one of her looks. Jake hunched his shoulders and looked up at me with sad eyes.

I squatted down to be eye level with my son. "Did you ask Mommy already?" I asked.

"Yes," Jake said quietly.

"Did she say no?"

"Yes."

"There's your answer, little man." I looked at Jake sternly. "Don't do that again," I said, knowing he would the next chance he got.

Jake looked down. "Okay."

"Take my coat to the closet, Jake. And when you're done, look in the pocket. You might find something for you," I said.

Jake grabbed my coat and ran to the closet, dragging it across the floor. He fairly threw it in the small space, and then rummaged the pockets. When he found the small car I had in there, he squeaked and ran back to his room, where he pulled out a small box full of little cars. My coat never made it further than the floor. Oh, well.

I kissed Sarah and placed a gentle hand on Aaron's head. His eyes never opened as he continued with his bottle, his little mouth working to get as much in his belly as possible.

"Hey, you," Sarah said. "How did you meeting with Charlie go?"

I stretched and rolled my head back. "Badly."

"Oh, dear. How many?"

"Forty-three," I said quietly.

"Oh my God. What happened?" Sarah shifted, and Aaron answered with a small burp, then he kept going.

"Ambushed from behind by a crowd of middle-schoolers. Nothing anyone could have done," I said. "We'll be into Cedar Rapids tomorrow."

Sarah nodded. Then she turned her very green eyes on me. "John, is this worth it? I mean, I know you're in this to make sure Jake and Aaron and all the other kids can grow up without looking over their shoulder all the time, but my god, if we take more losses like that, we won't have an army. And I don't mean from death by zombie."

I thought about it. "It has to be, Sarah. We have to be the ones to do it. There's no one else. No one I know about, anyway. Besides, what happened today shouldn't happen again. We have a plan, and we'll get it done."

"How long will we be on the road?" Sarah asked.

"I don't know," I said, honestly. "If I had another twenty thousand fighters, I would guess a year. But with what we have now? Maybe two, possibly three." I looked carefully at Sarah. "Are you wanting to head home? If you are, just say so, and I'll get a driver and an escort tomorrow to get you and the boys back to Starved Rock."

"I didn't say that," Sarah said quickly. "My place is with you. But I worry about bringing Jake and Aaron into the war."

"Me, too. But they are as safe here as anywhere, and I'd rather you were with me than at home. There's no one I'd rather have my back than you," I said.

Sarah smiled. She shifted Aaron and held him to her shoulder. A few small pats, and a very satisfied burp came from him. I was always amazed that such a large sound could come from such a small person. She rocked him gently, and I could see his eyes close and his body relax against his mother.

"I'll put this guy to bed if you want to put the other one to bed as well," Sarah said, moving to the front of the trailer to put Aaron in his crib.

"On my way." I got up and walked back to the rear of the trailer where Jake had his bed. There was room for a queen-sized bed back there, but since we didn't need all that room, we put in a couple of storage units, and Jake slept on a bunk on the far wall. His bed was attached to the top of two dressers, one that held his clothes, and the other his toys. He was in the middle of the room playing with his cars when I came in.

"Bedtime, shorty," I said, gathering up some of his toys.

"I'm not tired," Jake said automatically.

"Don't have to be; you just have to go to bed," I said, just as automatically.

"Mmmm," Jake grumbled as he climbed the little ladder to his bed. He tumbled into the bedding, covering himself with his blankets. He curled into a ball and turned away from me, another way he expressed his displeasure with going to bed early. I leaned over, and kissed his head anyway for no other reason than to irritate him a little further. He hunched even deeper under the covers, and I left his room with a smile.

I put the rest of my gear away and made my way to the master bedroom. It was a big room, even for a trailer, but it wasn't the biggest I could have chosen. There were trailers in our midst that had two floors for sleeping quarters—they were that big. I had no use for anything of that size, and by the time the boys were big enough to argue over separate rooms, I hoped to be living back at the lodge where they could have dozens of rooms to choose from.

I took off most of my clothing and settled into the bed next to Sarah. I put my arms around her, and she slipped back into me, molding her body next to mine. We lay like that for a long time, and I listened to her breathing become slow and more regular. I was drifting off to sleep myself when I heard something quiet but insistent.

"Daddy! Daddy!"

I sighed. Jake could be a big pain in the ass when it came to going to sleep. Sometimes he played these games. I was tempted to ignore him and let him figure it out when he did it again.

"Daddy!" It was a little louder, and he squeaked a little. That was different. I was fully awake now, and I could sense Sarah was as well.

"What's wrong?" Sarah could likely feel the tension in me as I listened to the darkness.

"I don't know. Watch Aaron." I slipped out of bed and quickly put my jeans on. I had no trouble facing danger without a shirt, but it was weird without pants of some sort. I tucked my Glock into the back pocket, grip inward for a quicker draw. Some people liked reverse appendix carry, but I never was comfortable sweeping myself with my own gun.

I moved quietly down the trailer and into Jake's room. Jake was huddled into a ball under his covers, and I could tell he was nervous because he jumped when I touched him.

"Daddy?" the little mound whispered again.

"I'm here, Jake. Daddy's here. Daddy's got you. What's wrong?" I looked around and didn't see anything that could have spooked him.

"I saw a man outside," Jake said, pointing a little hand towards the windows at the rear of the trailer. From Jake's vantage point, he could see out the windows that he normally couldn't when he was on the floor.

"Probably just a guard, Jake; they're supposed to be there. They keep us safe."

"No! I seen his eyes!"

"His eyes, Jake? How could you see his eyes in the dark?" I asked.

"Shining eyes!" Jake said.

Aw, hell. We had a zombie in the perimeter. I scooped up Jake and brought him to the front of the trailer.

Sarah was waiting for us, and Jake slipped into her arms. I answered the question in her eyes.

"Outside. I'll be a minute. May have an unwanted guest," I said.

"Please be careful," Sarah said. She ran a hand over Jake's hair while her other hand checked the proximity of her gun. She liked the Glock 19 for fieldwork since we could swap mags and ammo, but for home defense she had her baby which was a stainless SIG X-5. The gun fit her hand like a glove and had a sweet trigger. Sarah could hit a two-inch target all day long at forty yards with that gun.

I put my coat back on and put my Glock in the cabinet. I couldn't risk firing a gun with all the trailers that were around me, so I'd have to do this the old-fashioned way. I took out my pick and my bowie, hoping I'd not need either, but I had a feeling it was going to come to that. I put on a long sleeve shirt and my vest, giving myself some protection against the cold. Boots and gloves came next, and then I was out the door.

I stepped away from the vehicle and circled wide to the rear, trying to figure out which way the zombie might have gone that Jake saw. I didn't doubt he saw something, and he had seen enough of the real thing to know it when he saw it. I was grateful he had enough sense not to start screaming and draw the thing right to us. As much as I hated hunting Z's in the dark, this was preferable to having one of the stupid things bang on your trailer trying to get in.

The sky was overcast, and it was dark as hell. Out in the wild, without any ground lights, it got very black. Things were quiet in the camp which explained why the zombie was just wandering through. As far as he was concerned, I was sure, this was just a weird forest of metal that happened to be in his way.

I moved quietly around the trailer and looked at the area where Jake had seen his monster. I didn't bother checking for any tracks since hundreds of feet had passed this way. I thought about making some kind of noise, but I figured that would make me the subject of the hunt, not the zombie. I thought about where it might have gone when I heard someone laughing about a hundred feet from where I was. Bingo. If I heard it, the ghoul heard it, and he would go in that direction. I moved quietly, keeping away from the trucks, trailers, and campers that covered the landscape. I didn't want to be surprised by a ghoul that suddenly came out from underneath a trailer or something.

Walked quietly, checking behind me, and searching for glowing eyes. That was the only thing that made hunting zombies at night palatable. Fun part was, not all of their eyes glowed. Most of them, but not all. Truth was, it was creepy as hell.

I listened carefully and thought I heard a sound further down the lane. It sounded like a soft scrape on asphalt, and it was not repeated, like someone was trying to be quiet. I hoped to God they weren't evolving enough to try sneaking up on people. That would be just plain unfair.

I moved quietly, and ducking around a trailer, I got a glimpse of a dark shape moving silently through the encampment. It moved slowly, glancing from side to side. I heard the laughter again, but this time it was behind me. The zombie in front of me should have turned around, but he didn't.

That wasn't normal. As I watched, the shape moved quietly towards a trailer and looked inside a window before moving on. That wasn't right either. All evidence I was seeing was telling me this wasn't a zombie, but a live person.

I was about to challenge whoever they were when they suddenly turned around to check their back. I was between two trailers, so I just stepped back out of sight. But I managed to see the man's eyes, and that explained what Jake had seen. The man was wearing some sort of goggles, and they glowed pale green in the night.

Not something any of our men used. We'd tried night vision goggles before, but they were limited in what they could be used for, and the men preferred flashlights, anyway.

I moved around the other side of the trailer and up front as quickly as I could, trying to get in front of the man. I wanted to stop him without killing him, since he was clearly not from our camp. When I reached the point I wanted, I turned into the lane, and looked for the man to approach. A quick glance, showed me...nothing.

Shit, he moved. He didn't come out my side, so he had to have gone out the other side. I moved across the lane and through the line of RV's on the other side. As I crossed to the other side, I ducked suddenly and rolled forward as a stabbing blade skimmed over my back. I jumped forward and spun around, facing the man with the glowing green eyes. He was holding a long bladed knife and held it like he knew what to do with it.

I shifted my bowie to my left hand while I lengthened the hold on my pick. That gave me another ten inches of reach, and the move wasn't lost on the intruder. He stepped back and then jumped forward, his left hand reaching for my pick while his knife stabbed towards my throat.

I wasn't going to give up that easily. I flipped my pick under his grasping hand and held it straight out, holding tight as he ran into the metal end with his mouth. His knife never got closer than eight inches as he fell back holding his teeth. I swung low for his knee, and as he stepped back out of the way, I stopped the pick and jabbed it upwards again, connecting with the goggles on his face. His head jerked back, and he ripped the eyepieces off, blinking as his eyes adjusted to the darkness.

"Who are you?" I asked, waving my bowie back and forth. My pick I kept between us, using it as a barrier against his attacks.

"We're not here to hurt you; we're here to clear the zombies away. Who are you?" I repeated. The man stepped back and bumped against a trailer.

Suddenly, the man cut down viciously, and I easily blocked the attack with my handle. The sharp blade cut deep, and stuck in the wood. I twisted the handle away, taking his weapon with it, and brought my knife to bear, but the man had already let go and was running away into the night.

"What the hell?" I asked out loud to nobody. I gave chase, but the man zigzagged through the encampment and out to the prairie. I let him go since I had no idea if he was alone, and I was loathe to raise a general alarm. I started the long walk back to my trailer, and back by the first encounter, I knocked something with my feet. Reaching down, I found it was the goggles the man had worn. Apparently he had dropped them in his hurry to get away.

I went back to my trailer and stashed the items safely, figuring out what I wanted to do with them in the morning. I took Jake back to his bed, telling him he was a good boy for getting me, and yes, I did get the monster-guy. Sort of.

Sarah was relieved I was back safe and sound, and I told her I would talk to her about it in the morning. I tried to get some sleep, but it was a long time coming.

The next day, I took my pick with the knife still stuck on it and went over to Charlie's trailer. After the usual morning greetings, I showed Charlie my items and told him what had happened last night. He was mad for a few reasons, not the least of which at me for not coming to see him last night. The other thing he was mad about was the fact that our security was bad enough that a man had gotten through without so much as a challenge from anyone before he was wandering around the camp. I didn't bother to add that had it been a zombie we'd be in a world of crap right now with newly infected people to put down.

"Let's deal with a few things first. Get the burial crew going, and we'll have our service this morning. After that, let's get the people in charge of security here, and we'll talk to them as well. We have a city to retake, and this can wait till later," I said.

Charlie didn't like it, but he figured I was right. We needed to deal with internal issues first before we dealt with external.

About an hour later, I was standing in front of a series of graves, all marked with the names of the fallen. Sarah was behind me, and Tommy and Duncan were there as well. About a thousand people showed up for this service, and all of them were sad by the loss of their friends.

I started by reading the 23rd Psalm, then I spoke for a few more minutes. I didn't bother with any clichés or talking about the greater good. I just spoke about how these were people who fought for a cause they believed in, and in this cause, sometimes we died. It was a damn shame, but it was the truth.

After the burial, Charlie and I went back to the campaign office where we called in the security detail from the night before. There were questions we wanted answered.

Four men and two women stood before us. I brought out my pick with the knife still in it and the night vision goggles. I got right to the point.

"The pick is mine. The other two items came off a man who was in camp last night uninvited and obviously unchallenged by anyone on duty last night," I said. "I'm not going to waste time with scary stories of what ifs. He got in, he got out. The only reason we knew he was there was because my son happened to see him outside our trailer."

Charlie chimed in. "And he tried to kill John. Anyone want to start off, or should we just chalk this one up to stupid, and let you guys deal with it?"

One man stepped forward. "Our apologies, sir. Won't happen again."

Charlie looked at him for a full minute before answering. "Apology accepted. You will deal with this lapse, and if anything like this happens again, you will all be sent back to the capital to spend the rest of the war trying to explain to your families and friends why you are there and we are here. Understood?"

The threat of public shaming was very real to these people, and none of them wanted to face their peers for screwing up so badly.

"Dismissed," Charlie said. None of the six had the guts to look me in the eye. I was angry, but my anger was diminishing at the mystery we had in front of us.

"Who do you think it was?" I asked.

Charlie shrugged. "No idea. Could be a lone survivor who spent too much time alone or someone part of a larger group trying to figure out who the hell we are."

"Both viable options. Would that I could have secured him for questioning," I said.

"Wishful thinking," Charlie responded. "You know as well as I do there isn't anything worse than a man wanting very badly to leave someplace. Remember that guy in Oak Forest back home? He practically crawled up a vent shaft to get away. Nothing was going to stop him."

"No kidding. If he had to eat through a brick wall, that would not have stopped him. Changing the subject, are we ready for the assault on Cedar Rapids?" I asked.

"Just about. We need to get the three groups in place, but that shouldn't take more than an hour. Where do you want to be with this one?" Charlie asked.

"I'll take the group from the north. We'll clear the suburbs out on that end while the earth-movers take care of boxing in the city," I said.

"Good enough. I'll be on the East side, and Tommy will take the Southern end. Duncan will be working with the earth movers, and he wants you to know he has a few ideas he'd like to bounce off of you," Charlie said.

"Do you know what these ideas might be?" I asked with more than a little trepidation in my voice.

"I do, but I'm going to keep still to see if you have the same reaction I did," Charlie said.

"I'm so lucky to have a friend like you," I said.

"Yes, you are."

"Go kill something, will you?"

"Yes, sir."

An hour and a half later I was on the north side of Cedar Rapids fully geared up and looking for trouble. The homes looked like the same kind of homes you would find in any other city or suburb. It really struck me how much the country looked alike once you stopped for a minute and seriously took a good look at everything around you.

Four fighters were with me, and we were the point of our group, walking into infected territory and setting up the zombies for killing. Behind us was a battalion of fighters going into homes and killing zombies. Behind them was another battalion bringing in support for the first battalion. The third battalion was cleanup and catalog. Any usable supplies were taken by the third group, and anything we didn't need we just left. Others in the area might need what we left behind.

The drill was constant. Hit the door, open it, and back away. Usually we had the chance to put some distance between us and the infected coming out to say hi, but sometimes we didn't.

I was back with the other four while the door opener, a hulking brute of a lad, kicked the door in to a small ranch house on what would have been a very nice street. Even under the dead grass and the trees still holding on to their morning frost in their shaded areas, the suburb seemed like it would have been a good place in different times. Wide lanes for cars, and tree-lined easements with many wooded lots gave the impression this once was a well-to-do section of town.

"Back up, Sam!" barked the squad's leader. Steve Mendez was a tough man to please, but he kept his squad alive.

Sam dodged back as three zombies worked their way to the front of the house. A man, a woman, and a teenage girl all came slowly out of the house. They moved stiffly, as if the act of walking hurt them, but they kept coming anyway. The man looked to be in the best shape, while the two women were ripped and torn. The mother's gut was torn open, and I could see she was missing a few organs. It didn't take too much imagination to figure out who had turned first and then turned on the others.

Steve took out the man, cleaving his skull with an axe handle that had two spikes driven through it. Sam took the teenager down, just slamming a knife through the top of her skull. I killed the third, using a side swing and the pointed end of my pick to let her rejoin her family in the afterlife.

"Keep moving, get to the next house!" Mendez said.

We moved to the next house, and this time it went more smoothly. We came, we knocked, we got away. It was a pattern that worked for us most of the time, however, there were forty-three graves that proved it wasn't foolproof. We just kept going, up one street, and then the next. Behind us came the sounds of combat and death. We used the zombie's tactics against him. Where he once had the superior numbers, now we faced them two or three to one, and we avoided the major confrontations. We weren't going to win those, anyway. The cities we left alone, hemming in the zombies and leaving them there. If anyone wanted something from the city after it was closed off, he was welcome to try it. But don't expect any sympathy when the mission failed.

Down the third street we found a house that was different. It was boarded up tight with just a little space on the top of each window. The doors were sealed shut, and I could see wedges had been pounded into place all around the door. Not even three Sam's and a Charlie could kick that door open. It was a small, two-story house, the kind that a new family bought when they were just starting out. I walked around the house and saw the same situation in the rear. Locked up tighter than a drum, and zombies surely weren't getting in.

I looked up into the second story and saw that there were blinds drawn on all the upstairs windows. On the roof, a well-maintained windmill spun silently, its gear shaft disappearing into the roof below. If I had to bet, I'd say there was a small hand-cranked generator in there that was supplying a tiny bit of power to the house.

"Moving on, sir?" Steve asked. He looked up at the windmill and scowled.

"May as well," I said. Whoever is in there isn't going to open up for us, and if they've lived this long, they'll figure out its safe sooner or later."

We kept moving throughout the day, stopping briefly to eat something before pressing on. I took my turn at the door kicking, and things went reasonably well. We advanced around the city and stopped when we reached the point where Charlie's group started. That was it for the day.

"Sir! It's time we headed back to the camp, sir. Second battalion is cleaning up here." Mendez was somewhat anxious, and I wasn't sure why.

"All right. You go on ahead, I'm going to see if I can't find some high ground and have a look over the area," I said.

"Sir, do you want an escort?" Mendez took his duties seriously, and usually that meant keeping me out of harm's way. I wasn't having any of it today.

"I think I might be able to handle myself; thanks anyway," I said, probably a little more forceful than I should.

"Sir. As you wish, sir. Do you wish for me to inform anyone, sir?"

"Do that and I'll be very disappointed in you, Mendez."

"Understood, sir."

I walked out of the subdivision and started looking up. Off in the distance was a water tower, one of the larger ones. While I would have preferred a building of some sort, I wasn't about to go looking for one. Sometimes you just had to work with what the Lord provided, relatively speaking.

I started in the direction of the tower, and the direct path was going to take me through another subdivision. I was okay with that, since I figured this one had been taken care of as well. The doors on most of the houses had been opened, and here and there were the remains of the former occupants. When we killed them, we laid them out in neat rows so anyone coming behind us would know they were killed by us. Anything that was not orderly was usually an indication that we had not been through there yet, and one needed to proceed with caution.

I walked down the middle of the street, and it was quiet enough that I let my mind drift a little. I thought about the road we were on and what it took to get here. As usual, I had my doubts, but when I looked at the big picture what else was I supposed to do? There was an old saying that in order for evil to survive, good men must do nothing. Well, the ghouls were an evil, and I wasn't going to do nothing.

I walked along, keeping an eye out for the tower, and that was when I heard it. It wasn't much of a sound, like someone trying to suppress a sob. I stopped my movement and closed my eyes, focusing on trying to hear another sound and finding its location. It was a bit ironic that the zombies did kind of the same thing, only for some reason their hearing was better than ours.

There. To my left, maybe in a house. I walked in that direction, straining my ears for another sound that would lead me in the right direction. If it was a survivor, I needed to find them. If it was a zombie tactic, it was the best one I had seen so far, and I was falling right for it.

There it was again. This time it wasn't a sob, it was more of a snarl of anger or frustration. I looked around and didn't see anyone, so I went up to the split-level that seemed to be the source of the noise. The door was open, and I moved in, my bowie out in my left hand, while my right held my Glock.

"Rrrr!"

That sound was loud, and it sounded very, very angry. Knowing my luck, I was about to free some mutant Chihuahua that was going to tear my ankles apart. Zombies I could handle. Freaked out little dogs drove me nuts.

I moved up the stairs and stopped as I saw a pair of boots. They were facing away from me, and as I looked up I could see one of our fighters looking into a bedroom. I could hear muted voices and a low whistle. Right away I had a bad feeling. I needed to get the lookout away from the door, and I needed something strange to get his attention. Pulling out my canteen, I sprinkled a little water on my hand. Stepping around the corner, I flipped water droplets at the man.

It took three tries, but finally the man stepped away, coming down the stairs, and looking up at the ceiling. I waited until he was in front of me before I grabbed the back of his neck with my left hand while my right held the bowie to his throat.

The man's eyes were huge, and when he recognized me, they got even bigger.

"How many?" I asked.

The man shook, causing my blade to bite his neck a little. He held up two fingers.

"Anyone hurt yet?" I asked.

The man shook his head ever so slightly.

I whipped the knife away and brought the hilt crashing down on the top of his head. The man slumped, and I had to act quickly to keep his falling body from making too much noise. I cut his shoelaces to make makeshift cuffs and then headed back to the stairs. I didn't waste any time; I just took the steps in stride, and at the top of the stairs brought my gun to bear on the scene in front of me.

Three of our fighters were in there, two men and a woman. One of the men was holding the woman by the arms, pinning them back and keeping her from moving. Her shirt was open, and one breast was already exposed. Sitting on her feet with a knife in his hand was the other man. He was systematically cutting away her pants from her legs, one strip at a time. The woman couldn't move, and a dish towel had been stuffed in her mouth, keeping her from expressing the obvious rage I could see in her eyes.

"I'd say this violates most of the rules we have for conduct in the army," I said. "Let her go." I commanded, pointing the gun directly at the face of the man holding the woman. The man on the floor shifted, and I kicked him hard in the head, knocking him over. His knife slid out of his hand as his head bounced off the floor.

The man holding the woman released his grip, and I had to give the woman credit. She didn't even bother to cover up or take the gag out of her mouth. She just spun around and slammed a fist into the side of the man's throat, putting him on the ground, and causing him to gasp for air.

After that she took the gag out and threw it on the man on the ground. She covered herself and fastened her coat over her torn top. There wasn't much she could do with the pants, so I helped her take the pants off the man I had kicked, and she put those on.

"Thank you, sir," the woman said.

"What happened? What's your name?" I asked. I already knew what happened at the end, I was curious as to how the story got there.

"Melissa. Melissa Durant, sir," she answered. "These two were in my squad, and when we cleared this house asshole here grabbed me, and the other two just went along."

I looked at Melissa, and I could see why men would be attracted to her. She was a pretty brunette with short hair and light brown eyes. She picked up her pack and slung it on. When she looked up her eyes got huge.

I spun around, bringing my Glock to bear. The man I had taken down on the lower level had returned, and he was coming through the doorway like a charging bear. I fired point blank into his chest, stopping him cold. He took a step back, and placed a hand on his heart. The awful realization of what had just happened to him turned his face ashen, and then he fell to the floor.

I shrugged at Melissa. "Guess that saves us the trouble of a trial," I said. I turned to the men on the ground. "Get up, or I'll shoot you next."

The men got up painfully but cooperated. I marched them out of the house ahead of me, and our little procession headed back to the camp. Outside, I had Melissa cover the men while I switched from my Glock to my rifle. If the men had any notion of being able to get away while I held a handgun on them, that notion vanished when I held my rifle.

We got back to camp, and I handed the two men off to Steve Mendez. He didn't even want to know why one of the men wasn't wearing pants. He just put them under guard and left them in the cold. I aimed Melissa over to the medical center and ordered her to be checked out. Next I found Tommy and told him what had happened, and after a brief discussion, he went over to the medical center to talk to Melissa.

I found Charlie a little while later, and he was in the process of getting reports from squads about zombie encounters and numbers. I gave him a brief on the situation, and he looked grim, but nodded. Finishing that, I went outside and realized I had never gotten to my vantage point. Oh, well. It was a moot point now, anyway. I walked back toward my trailer, checking my rifle in the process. One of the scope mounts seemed loose, so I stopped to give it a little tighten.

Figuring I had lost my zero, I now had something to do. I walked to my trailer and called for Sarah to come out.

"What's up?" Sarah's beautiful face popped out of the trailer just inches from mine. I took advantage of the opportunity and gave her a quick kiss, which she returned enthusiastically after her surprise.

"My rifle's scope came loose, can you sight it back in for me?" I asked. "I'll watch the boys."

"Deal. Jake has been a little difficult today." Sarah popped back into the trailer, and I followed. She shrugged her coat on and took my rifle from me.

"I'll deal with him. He's probably just bored," I said, taking my coat off and putting my gear away.

"There is that. When are we done here?" Sarah asked, heading for the door.

"Tomorrow we should be ready to move; the earth movers should be done today and loaded by tomorrow morning," I said.

"Good. I like it better when we're on the move," Sarah said, stepping outside.

"Me, too" I said, to no one in particular.

A half an hour later, Sarah came into the trailer. She handed me the rifle and nodded. "Two hundred yard zero, you weren't far off. By the way, out by the range, there was a man with binoculars studying the camp. He scampered off when I started sighting in."

I was suddenly very interested. "You don't say. Too bad you didn't get a round his way. Might have scared him off for good." I was thinking about my encounter the other day and wondered if it might be the same man.

"Thought about it, but he was gone before I could get a bead on him," Sarah said. "Anything else happen today besides your rifle being out of whack?"

I told her about the encounter today with Melissa, and Sarah's eyes narrowed, but she kept quiet. I knew she was completely okay with whatever I decided to dish out to the two men, but as I had time to think it over, I realized we only had one real course of action.

"What are we going to do to these men?" Sarah asked.

"Unfortunately, we can't do what we would really like to do. Are they guilty of attempted rape? Yes. Are they guilty of rape? Probably at some point in the past, yes. But right now, no," I said. "And before you jump on me, think about it first." I could see the storm building in Sarah's eyes, and I was trying to head it off.

To her credit, Sarah did think first, and I knew precisely when she reached the same conclusion I had. These men would be dealt with, but we couldn't mete out the justice they likely deserved.

I gave Sarah a hug. "Don't worry. It will be fine."

The road crews finished the encircling of the city sooner than expected, and Duncan was very pleased with himself as he presented his report. I took the reports from the other commanders and then had a brief meeting about our two offenders from the day before. As much as we wanted to hang the two of them, it wasn't in the cards. I didn't want to keep them prisoner since I didn't want to waste resources on them. Tommy came up with the best answer, which suited me just fine. We would banish them upon pain of death should they ever return to any populated area.

In the morning, I held a brief meeting with the two men and the rest of my commanders. I had each commander take a very long look at each man, and then sat everyone down. The two men I left standing.

"I'll keep this short. I never was long on speeches, and I had hoped never to give this one. You two are a disgrace to humanity. I am sure that had I not intervened, you would be guilty of at least rape and then likely murder since a witness would turn you in. But I didn't catch you at rape. I caught you at attempted rape. "I said. "Lucky for you, because if I had caught you in the act of rape, I would have killed you both right then."

"As it is, you are hereby banished, never to return to any community within the New United States. You will be taken to a place outside the jurisdiction of the laws of the Constitution to fend for yourself as best you may."

I continued. "You will not be given any supplies save for the clothes on your backs. As you cared so little for the well-being of a fighter sworn to protect you in battle, we will care as much for you. Should you try to rejoin the New United States, you will be executed on the spot."

I turned to Charlie. "Deputy Chief Executive, do you have a place in mind for the banishment of these men?"

Charlie stood. "Yes, sir." He signaled to the door, and four men entered followed by six women fighters, one of whom was Melissa Durant. Her face was a mask, and her eyes cold as she approached the men. The four men took the two prisoners and marched them out of the room, followed by the women.

"Where's the nearest place outside our jurisdiction, deputy?" I asked.

"That would be the city of Cedar Rapids, sir." Charlie said.

"That will do," I replied. "Throw them over the wall. Let them try and rape the zombies over there." It wasn't necessarily within the law, but it was justice, nonetheless.

MONTANA
CENTER MOUNTAINS

"Report."

The word was ripe with meaning, and none of it boded well. The speaker was a large man, over six feet with heavy, sloping shoulders. His calloused hands were clasped in front of him, resting easily on the oak table he sat behind. His muscular arms strained at the confines of his shirt, and his large head was topped with dark brown hair streaked with grey. His face was scarred from several battles over the course of the last three years, yet his deep blue eyes had lost none of their fire. He looked like a mature panther, waiting for his moment to strike. His pose was casual, yet he was capable of explosive movement at any time.

Cole Hobbes was a simple man once upon a time. He had worked in the trades most of his life, starting out as a bricklayer with his father when he was just sixteen. Long days of work had filled him out, and the rough and tumble bars his father eventually brought him to had taught him many things about life he had never learned in school or on the job. By the time he was in his forties, he had buried his father, gotten married and had a son, and basically looked forward to the day when he could teach his son about the value of a hard day's work.

All that changed when the Upheaval hit. Cole had been different from his contemporaries, taking advantage of what the Internet had to offer when his son had shown him the way. On the web he found reports and sightings; things that didn't make sense. He'd seen the end coming long before others had, and when the end finally arrived, he was already on his way to a safe haven, family in tow.

He'd secured a decent sized cabin in the wilds of Montana and set about making sure his family was safe. Heather Hobbes never questioned her husband and was grateful every day that her family was still together after so many had lost so much.

Cole had sent a simple message to his friends and coworkers. 'Heading to the wild, here's the coordinates.' Cole never expected anyone to arrive, but in the months after the upheaval, they began to trickle in. Men with skills; men used to working with their hands. Men who figured out problems that CEO's couldn't ever get in a decade of trying. Society used to look past these men, never noticing them until needed. Here they found their friends and brother tradesmen. Here they built a society with their bare hands. Here they created a haven from the wild ghouls that had torn so many others apart. And here, Cole Hobbes was the leader of them all.

"We've expanded the outer perimeter, expanding the wall well past the canyon. There's useful timber in the hills and the cleared fields will be helpful for additional crops. There are two solid rock hills that the electricians want to use for the foundation of their windmills, and they think they can help the plumbers get more water up from the streams."

Cole grunted. The electricians were goddamned magicians when it came to power, once they were allowed to let their imaginations run free. The hardest part was getting them the parts they needed to make it all work. Every home had electric power, and no one was cold in the winter months. One of the lunatics had built an electric sidewalk that kept snow off of his walkway.

"Good enough. We could use the timber and the land," Cole said. "Anything else?" Cole said.

The advisor, a small man named Darnell Tibbles, had been a welder before the end of the world. He'd known Cole from the old days and had come along a week after Cole had left. Darnell was an unassuming man, and both he and Cole had been surprised as hell to find that Darnell the Welder was also remarkably organized and efficient at administration. They often joked with each other that had Darnell figured out his secondary skills sooner, he'd have been a rich man with his own welding company.

"Not on the domestic front," Darnell said. "On the other end, I heard something you might be interested in."

Cole shifted his head slightly towards Tibbles.

"Do tell."

"One of the survivors we found wandering the outer perimeter had said something strange before we relocated him," Darnell said.

"Spit it out, I've got no patience for stories," Cole said.

"He said the army will be here soon," Darnell said.

Cole shook his head. "Crazy talk. The army's been finished for years. Even those state centers they set up are done."

"True enough."

Cole straightened his back and popped his neck before speaking.

"But?"

"But what if there's another army?" Darnell asked.

Cole shook his head. "None that could get us here. We're surrounded on three sides by canyons, and the other side is a sheer mountain. Trust me, we're fine from man, beast, or zombie."

"Well, just to be sure, I sent a couple of scouts out about three weeks ago to see if there was anything to it," Darnell said.

Cole stared at Darnell. "When were you going to tell me about this?"

"I just did."

Cole stood up, towering over Darnell. He raised a large fist and held in front of Darnell's pale face.

"I think I need to remind you who is in charge here. I'm the one who started this place, not you. Are we clear?" Cole said.

Darnell took a step back. "Crystal. I will try and recall the men."

"Leave them. If they die out there, it's on you to provide for their families. Period," Hobbes said with finality. Tibbles knew better than to argue. Inwardly, he was cursing himself for bringing it up at all.

"Dismissed," Cole said, sitting back down. The wooden chair creaked in protest as the full weight of the large man bore down upon it.

Darnell Tibbles left the meetinghouse and headed out toward the canyon rim. He passed several houses and walked down the narrow road of the small town at the base of the mountain.

As he passed a corner, a voice halted him.

"Evening, Tibbles."

Darnell looked over at the speaker. He was a young man, tall and strong. His broad shoulders were accented by his narrow hips, and his arms were long and powerful. He somehow had managed to get the best of both his parents. The strength of his father combined with the good looks of his mother.

Darnell didn't like the look in the young man's eye so he decided to play it safe.

"Good evening, Carson. How are you?" Tibbles said, careful to strike a neutral tone with his boss' son.

"Oh, passable. Just passable," Carson Hobbes said smoothly. He let his eyes drift out over the canyon, allowing a full minute to pass before he asked his question.

"So, what did my father say about the scouts?" Carson was actually the one who sent the men out; Darnell had covered for him, and they both knew it. Carson wasn't yet ready to challenge his father's authority, but he wasn't above letting others take the heat if he could convince them it was worth their while.

Darnell whistled softly. "He wasn't happy, that was for sure. Next time I'll let you take the blame."

Carson gave Darnell a half smile. "Now, Tibbles, you know that almost sounds like you want to back out of our deal."

"Deal?" Tibbles snorted. "You didn't give me much choice, did you?"

Carson smiled again. "Well, you do have a pretty daughter. Maybe I should pay more attention to her after all."

Darnell's eyes turned cold. "I'd recommend against that kind of thing, Hobbes. I respect your dad and what he's done here, and me taking the blame for you isn't a big deal as far as that goes. But if you think you can back out of our deal, you'd best be ready to go all the way."

"You threatening me, Tibbles?" Carson's eyes lit up at the prospect of battle, and the only thing he wished for right now was an audience for him to fight in front of. He'd never lost a fight in his life, thrilling at the feel of landing blows on his opponents. But for all his fights, he'd never actually faced a zombie. He had been made safe too soon for that to happen, and others had done the fighting for him. It was the one thing he longed to do.

Darnell held out a hand. "Not at all. Just letting you know where I stand when it comes to you keeping your word."

Carson reached for the older man's hand. He'd teach him a lesson right now. Carson had a strong grip, and he liked to prove it whenever he shook hands. Grasping Darnell's hand, he gave a hefty squeeze.

Carson's grin fell off his face when his hand exploded in pain. His knuckles felt like they were being folded in half, and his fingers were suddenly numb. He very nearly fell to his knees when the pain stopped abruptly.

Darnell Tibbles gave Carson a smile of his own as he explained.

"What do welders do all day, son? They *grip* things and hold them steady. I've been a welder a long time, boy, and no one besides another welder could try that little game on me." Darnell winked at the young man. "Not even your dad would do that with me, boy. You do it again, and I'll crush your hand to a pulp."

Darnell whistled a little as he walked away, leaving a very hurt, but slightly wiser, Carson Hobbes behind.

Darnell kept walking, following the well-worn trails that wound through the community on the mountain. The paths were lit with small lanterns, and as he looked back, the great peak was covered in ropes of lanterns like a gigantic Christmas tree. Moving through the sparse trees, Darnell waved at folks who were sitting out on their porches, looking out at the incredible view they enjoyed every single day.

He kept walking, moving up the trails until he reached a small level area on the side of the mountain. It wasn't very big, but it was big enough for a small two- bedroom cabin that Darnell shared with his seventeen-year-old daughter, Alison. His wife had actually passed away from breast cancer ten years ago, and Alison was all he had. He'd been fortunate that his sister had helped him and Alison through the rough times of loss and Alison growing up, but she had been taken by the zombies in the first wave of the Upheaval.

The cabin was small but snug, and it was as comfortable as the two of them could make it. Darnell only wished for one thing in this world, and that was for Alison to find a good man to take care of her when he was gone.

Darnell walked through the door and immediately felt the tension in the air. It was a heavy feeling of dread, like something horrible had happened. Tibbles reached behind the clock on the wall and pulled out an old but cared-for Smith and Wesson revolver. It had been his father's when he had been a state trooper many years ago and had been in Tibbles' possession ever since he passed away.

"Alison?" Tibbles called out.

"In here, Dad!" Alison's voice didn't seem to have any danger in it, so Tibbles relaxed. He kept the gun, choosing to tuck it in his coat pocket as he walked over to the living room.

Darnell found Alison sitting in the living room talking to a man about twice her age. He was clean-shaven with a short haircut, and his clothing was pressed and clean. His Native American features went very well with his coal black eyes and hair, and there was a hint humor in his face that he claimed was part of his Irish heritage a couple of generations ago.

"Well, Luke Blacktail. What can I do for you?" Darnell asked of his visitor, shaking his hand as the man rose to greet him.

"Well, Mr. Tibbles, there is not much I need these days that requires welding," Luke said, smiling. His entire face changed when he smiled. His stern features melted away, and he seemed genuinely human. But his smile was gone in a minute when he became more serious.

"I do have a question I would like you to answer, if you would, please." Luke Blacktail sat back down, indicating that Darnell should do the same.

Darnell stood his ground. "I'll stand, and I'll excuse my daughter from this conversation." He waved a hand at Alison. "Why don't you head to your room, sweetheart? This won't take a minute."

"It might take a little longer than that, and she can stay," Blacktail said.

Darnell shook his head. "It won't. And neither will she. Please, honey. Into the other room." Darnell watched her leave the room, a worried look on her face.

Luke's eyes were hard. "You are a stubborn man, Mr. Tibbles."

Darnell's eyes were equally hard. "Learned it from our boss."

"That might be considered a dangerous thing to say," Luke said.

"Are we there, then? Have we reached the point where we are no longer a community but a kingdom?" Darnell asked.

Luke Blacktail leaned back and sighed. He'd had similar thoughts himself, and lately it seemed more often than not Cole Hobbes was acting more like a ruler than a leader.

"Not yet. But I caution you to choose your words with care around others," Blacktail said.

"I'm the soul of caution," Darnell said, with a smile of his own. "Now that we have that out of the way and know where we both stand, what was your question?"

Luke spoke softly. "What do you want me to do with the scout that came back?"

Darnell's heart suddenly leapt into his throat. He had no idea the men would return so soon. "He's actually here? He made it back? What about the other one?"

Luke shook his head. "Only one returned. He said they ran into some trouble in the Dakotas, and his partner was killed by some ghouls that surprised them one morning."

"That's too bad. Was he married?" Darnell explained his conversation with Col,e, regarding the care of any family members of the scouts.

"No, lucky for you. I have the other in a remote cabin right now. Cole doesn't know he's returned yet."

"Might have been good to know this before I gave my report just a little while ago."

"Not my worry. What is my worry is what he had to say," Luke said.

"Well, the day can't get worse," Tibbles said. "What did he report?"

As Luke Blacktail explained in detail what the scout had to say, Darnell Tibbles realized his day actually could, and did, get worse.

Half an hour later Blacktail left leaving Darnell standing on his porch. The sun had set while they were talking, and the night sky was in full bloom. Constellations and celestial bodies moved in a perpetual dance across the darkness. Darnell watched for a moment, thinking about what he had learned. The big decision now was what to do with the information. Did he bring it to Cole now, letting things fall where they may, or did he risk waiting to see what happened, knowing Cole's wrath should he ever find out that Darnell knew something and didn't reveal it? It was a gamble that Darnell wasn't sure he wanted to take. Had he been alone, it might have been easier, but since he had his daughter and her future to think about, it altered the equation.

The good news was he wasn't required to give another report for a week, so he had a day or so to think on his course of action. He also had to think about what was best for the community. Did he run the risk of a hostile takeover, or did he take his chances that the army the scout reported on was benevolent and would be good for the people at large?

In the end, Darnell decided that the best plan was to just report on what was seen, and let things fall where they may. If the army was as large as the scout had reported, then there wasn't much Cole Hobbes could do about it. If all of them were as good a shot as the one the scout talked about, there wasn't much Hobbes could do about that either. At least, that's what Darnell thought as the night grew darker and colder.

In the morning, Darnell walked back around the mountain and back to the main lodge. The community always looked different in the morning, and to Darnell's eyes, it just felt better. The row of homes that made up the main street were close together and represented the first families that had arrived behind Cole. After that space had been taken up, the rest spread out around the mountain. The core group kept to themselves, treating others a little differently, a little disdainfully. Tibbles never knew why, they were all tradesmen to some degree. Even the schoolteacher had been a journeyman carpenter.

The main lodge was a collection of buildings that happened to be built attached to each other. There was a meeting hall, a dining hall, a lounge that had a bar, and a small planning room. Cole liked to call it his 'ready room', although Darnell never could figure out why. Everything was built well, and built to last.

Darnell stepped inside the lodge and walked silently across the main hall. He headed towards the door that led to the Hobbes family cabin when voices in the Ready Room stopped him. He stepped over to the doorway, keeping out of sight. He could hear three distinct voices in there, and recognized them all.

"So the scout returned the other day? Funny Tibbles didn't mention it."

Darnell scowled. That would be Carson speaking, the little shit. *Should have broken his hand*, Tibbles thought to himself.

"He did not know until I visited him last night and gave him the news. So he could hardly be faulted for not wanting to tell you in the middle of the night."

Darnell's scowl deepened. Luke Blacktail was here selling him out! Son of bitch! Darnell's mind raced ahead trying to figure out what this meant.

"Well, we'll see what he does today. He's always been a loyal man, so I have no reason to doubt him now."

That was Cole. Darnell breathed a small sigh of relief when he realized Cole wasn't going to do anything stupid. But what was he to do now? If he walked in, they'd know he had been listening. The only thing he had to worry about was the other thing he and Luke had briefly spoken of.

He listened while Luke outlined what the scout had told him, and it was telling that Cole just let Luke talk without much bluster. In a way, that was actually more frightening. At the end of the description, Carson was the first to speak.

"What can they do to us here? We run this land, we own this mountain. We have our own army should it come to that. Let them come. I'll be happy to tell them to fuck off as I piss over the canyon rim at them," he said.

"I doubt it would come to that," Luke said. "But you have other things to watch for right here." Luke went on to discuss the controversial items he and Darnell had talked about the night before.

Darnell didn't bother to hear the end of the story. He retreated out of the lodge as quickly as he could and as silently as he could. Once outside, he bolted for his home, grateful that most people were still asleep at this early time. His progress wasn't as quick as he would have liked, for he slowed to walk by the houses that were next to the trial. He didn't want to give the appearance of anything being out of the ordinary.

It seemed like forever, but he finally reached his cabin. Getting inside, he was grateful his daughter was already awake and had finished her breakfast.

"Alison. Sweetheart. We need to leave, here. Now," Darnell said, going to the closet and pulling out two large backpacks.

Alison was confused. "What? Dad, why? What happened? Did you see Hobbes?"

Darnell stopped his packing to look Alison in the eye. "Luke was there, and he told Cole everything."

Inwardly, Alison groaned. She knew what loyalty meant to Cole and how difficult life would be for them here if word got out that Darnell was causing trouble. But *her* loyalty was to her father, and she immediately began pulling out canned and dried goods for their trip.

Darnell paused to take his daughter's hand. "I'm sorry it came to this, honey. It's my fault. I should have watched what I said," he said, sadly.

Alison gave her dad's hand a squeeze. "I was getting bored on this mountain anyway." She smiled and went back to her packing.

Darnell shook his head, grateful he had such a wonderful daughter. He wished briefly that his wife could have lived to see her now, but as he always reassured himself, her mother was always watching over them both.

They didn't have much, and in the end were able to get most of their belongings into the two packs. The rest they would have to leave. Darnell helped his daughter get her pack on, and she helped him with his. As they adjusted straps, Alison asked the question of the day.

"Which way do we go?"

Darnell smiled. He had been thinking about that since last night. "We get over the canyon, and we'll head southeast. Come on, let's head out the back and get to the east bridge. There shouldn't be anyone guarding it at this hour."

Alison turned out the lights and shut everything off. If anyone came within the next few minutes, it would look like they were still sleeping. It might buy them a few more minutes.

"Let's move!" Darnell led the way, leaving the cabin he had built behind. He didn't give it much thought, it was just a place to sleep and be alone. He'd find another. He worried a bit about Alison, but she was so much like her mother that he figured she'd be fine. She tended to take life as it came and not ask too much of anyone.

They worked their way through the back trails, avoiding the homes and cabins that spread out a little more. Further away from the main community, the homes were much farther apart, and the trees on the mountain provided decent cover for the fugitives. Darnell didn't know for sure that people were coming for him, but it suited him to be ahead of the game when it came to this.

As they walked, they kept their heads down and tried to move as quietly as possible. Darnell figured that if they could get over the East Bridge before the alarm was raised, they would be in great shape.

A half an hour later, they were finally at the East Bridge. Tendrils of mist rose from the canyon, caressing the steel work with vaporous fingers. The morning sun had not yet risen over the far mountains, so this area was still in a shade of night. Darnell was relieved to see that no one was guarding this side of the bridge.

"Okay, let's go. When we reach the other side, if there is a guard, you know what to do," Tibbles said.

"Right. You're not going to hurt anyone, are you?" Alison gave her father a stern look, one that on her pretty face was actually quite silly.

"No one I don't have to," Darnell promised.

The pair crossed the spooky bridge and on the other side expected to be challenged by a sentry. They looked around, but no one seemed to be in sight.

"That's weird," Darnell whispered. "Usually there's someone in the guardhouse right there."

Alison walked over and peered in. She came back with her report. "No one's in there," she said. "May as well keep moving."

"Good enough for me. Hopefully we can find a vehicle of some kind soon," Darnell said as the two of them walked down the road. On this side of the canyon, there were more of the community, but they busied themselves with expanding food fields and killing the occasionally nimble zombie.

Darnell wasn't kidding himself. Leaving the community meant leaving safety and security behind. Once they crossed the fence line, they were on their own in a big world full of ghouls.

The pair got ten yards towards freedom when a voice behind them stopped them both.

"Figured I'd find you here."

Darnell's heart sank as he heard that voice. He'd hoped there would have been more of a delay at the cabin and a general search through the community before they started covering exits.

Darnell turned around, keeping his hands in his pockets while he stepped in front of his daughter.

"Something I can do for you, Carson?" Tibbles asked casually.

"Where you headed, old man? This side of the canyon, there's monsters in the dark. Not so sure you can protect that daughter of yours." Carson smirked and adjusted the rifle he had slung over his shoulder. It was an old bolt-action rifle, but Darnell knew Carson could hit anything he wanted within one hundred yards. They'd never get away with him behind them.

"I'm leaving, Carson. The 'why' of it is none of your goddamned business," Darnell said.

"Well, you can leave. Your daughter has to stay," Carson said. "I won't ask you twice." The young man adjusted the rifle on his shoulder in a significant manner.

"No need." Darnell removed his hand from his pocket and drew out the revolver with it. He pointed it at Carson's midsection, and if he was honest with himself, he appreciated the look on Carson's face when he did so.

"Since we're out in the West, I believe the term is 'getting the drop on someone.' Well, boy, I'd say I have the drop and the advantage. Why don't you put that rifle on the ground and take about ten steps back?" Darnell said sternly.

Carson fumed, but there was nothing he could do. Deep down he was a bully and a coward, and as much as he would love to try a shot at Darnell, he didn't want to risk a bullet in the gut for it. He slipped the strap off his shoulder and very carefully put the rifle on the ground.

He backed up with his hands in the air, sneering as Alison picked up the rifle. She slipped it over her shoulder, giving Carson a disdainful look. Carson marked that look and swore to himself that if he ever had the chance, he'd make her pay for it. After he took care of her old man.

"Now what are you going to do, Tibbles? You shoot me, my father will chase you across the country to kill you," Carson said.

"That's true, and I don't really have it in me to kill the son of a man I considered my friend," Darnell said. "But I don't have too much trouble keeping him locked up for a while to give us a head start." Darnell pointed the gun at the guard shack and motioned for Carson to get inside. He sent his daughter get some small rocks and sticks.

When she returned, Darnell had his daughter cover the door while he secured the door with the rocks and sticks. Several sticks jammed in between the door and the frame was almost as good as a lock. Rocks jammed under the door worked just as well.

Carson watched from the small window, cursing at the pair the entire time. When he ran out of threats, he went over to swearing again, and then back to threats.

When he was done, Darnell spoke to Carson. "You can break out of here in about an hour, and then go running to your daddy. When you do, tell him I said not to follow me. It will go badly if I am followed. Leave me alone, and I'll not tell that army out there where to find you," he said. "You understand, you big pile of stupid?" Darnell didn't need to insult the man, but he'd swallowed enough from this punk to last a lifetime.

Carson answered by hitting the doorframe, rattling the shack. He cursed incoherently again.

"Let's go, Alison. The door will give way in about twenty minutes, and we need that time to get past the fence." Darnell picked his pack up, and the two headed east again. Darnell knew he was taking a huge risk, but there was nothing for him here anymore. Besides, with the way Carson and Cole were starting to act, Darnell was pretty sure more people might be looking for a change of scenery.

Hand in hand, Darnell and his daughter walked away from their home into uncertainty. Darnell had a plan, and if everything went well, he'd have his daughter safe within a few weeks.

If not, well, he had a plan for that, too.

SPRINGFIELD, MO

"Raise your hand if you like Missouri," Tommy said out loud to no one in particular.

"See? No one likes it here," Duncan said.

"You didn't even bother to see if anyone raised their hands," I complained.

"I didn't have to. This place is the pits. Trees, dirt roads, and God alone knowing what might be living in those homes we passed. How hard did the moron who called these tracks of dirt 'roads' hit his head before thinking it was a good idea?" Tommy said petulantly. "Anyone? What a mess."

"Not being one to point out the obvious," I said, daring Duncan to contradict me with an evil glare in his direction, "but weren't you the one with the map who declared this the best, most direct route through the state?"

"I will take partial blame for that, yes," Tommy said, steering around another fallen tree. "But I think another part of the blame lies with the man who was born here who chose to fall asleep when I was asking for directions!"

Three pairs of eyes descended upon Charlie's bulk as he dozed in the other captain's chair of the van we were using to scout ahead of the army. It was a wonder he didn't awake screaming from the scorch marks our eyes were trying to burn into him. To be charitable, he had been up all night. A zombie child had made it through our picket lines, and after the securing of people in their homes, Charlie went hunting. In the morning he finally came out of the weeds dragging a dead zombie. So while I could curse him for his directions, I wasn't going to wake him up to chastise him for it.

We'd cleared out Jefferson City and Columbia a week ago, and I had sent half of the remaining army to follow Interstate 44 and work on clearing the towns along that route. The way we worked it, the army spread out after a major offensive, casting themselves in a wide but travelling net thrown in the same direction. The goal was to clear out as much real estate as possible. One hundred four-man teams searched out every farmhouse and small towns as they made their way to a single goal: kill every zombie they find. For our part, we led a five hundred man team straight toward the objective to scout it out and see what resources we needed. We hit the bigger towns as well, which was why we were headed to Springfield. We'd then swing the entire army north to Kansas City and see what we could kill there.

Along the way, we picked up and lost parts of our army. It was the way I had wanted it when we started this campaign. I wanted to clear out the dead and replace them with living people to bring back the country as much as possible. If we came across a nice town that looked like it might have weathered the storm fairly well, some people elected to stay behind and rebuild. They knew they were on their own, but I wasn't too worried. Everywhere we went we left seasoned fighters that could stop an outbreak before it started. The people we picked up were survivors and fighters, usually looking to contribute to the new world we were building, but sometimes they were just looking for a change of scenery.

"Why up north?'"

"What? Did you say something?" I looked back from watching the forty millionth tree go by to refocus on something that was being said in my direction.

Duncan shook his head. "Why, yes, John, I did. Please pay attention next time." Duncan really played up the sarcasm, and it took a great deal of self-control not to kick the back of his chair.

"I'd listen more if you were more interesting," I said, trying to match his sarcasm. I must have succeeded, because Tommy chuckled.

"Anyway. What I said was why did you send nearly a quarter of our army north when winter is nearly upon us? We're heading south, and the zombies won't be frozen until much later," Duncan asked.

"Good question," I said. "It's a matter of timing. I am hoping that because the winter is already going on heavy up there, they can move much more quickly clearing out the zombies. The idea is to have them go through Minnesota, clear the Dakotas, and be through Montana before spring. By the time the snows are melting, they should be heading south. If all goes well, we should be moving up from the southwest at that time and meet them in the middle for the push across the middle states on our way back home."

Duncan looked back at me, and even Tommy took a quick look back.

"What?" I asked.

"I dunno, John. That's a hell of a lot of planning. Not exactly your strong suit. Wow!" Duncan said, lurching forward.

That time I did kick his seat.

"Hmm? Are we there yet?" Charlie murmured from his chair.

Tommy chimed in from the front. "Not yet. You just missed Climax Springs, which I'm sad to say wasn't, and we are having a hard time keeping the van on a road that refuses to stay a proper road."

Charlie took a look outside. "It will become road again on the other side of the creek. Keep going until you hit Macks Creek. Wake me then." With that, Charlie was out again.

I shook my head and looked back out the window. The trees were stripped bare of leaves, getting ready for the winter. The pine trees were green as always, and that kind of threw the whole picture off. I knew the southern states that made up the border between the north and the true south didn't get as much snow as the northern states did, but they got cold, and ice storms were frequent. Of course, we didn't have weathermen anymore. Nowadays weather forecasting consisted of looking out the window. Remarkably, we were right more often than the old weathermen seemed to be.

We left Charlie sleeping as we passed through Macks Creek and didn't bother him as we made it through Tunas and Buffalo. Both towns were very much alive, and we had good conversations with both of them. This just confirmed what I had always suspected; small town America was much better suited to survive a zombie apocalypse than any major city.

Tommy eased up when we reached 65, and it was pretty smooth going to Fair Grove. Charlie woke up just as we reached the outskirts of the town.

"This isn't Macks Creek," he said, rubbing his eyes and looking around.

"Nope, we made it all the way to Fair Grove," Duncan said, looking at his map. "We figured you could use the sleep."

"Not that I don't appreciate it, but I would have liked to have been awakened when we reached Macks Creek," Charlie said.

"Not to be a pain, but why?" Duncan asked. "The towns all look alike around here."

"My first wife and daughter are buried there. I would have liked to have paid my respects," Charlie said quietly.

"Aw, hell, Charlie, I'm sorry," Duncan said. "We can stop by on the way back if that would work." Duncan sounded genuinely sorry.

Tommy nodded. "Not a problem at all, bro. I'm used to the roads; we'll get back there in no time. You can have a nice long visit."

Charlie looked sad, but grateful. "Thanks, guys, it would mean a lot to me."

We got out of the van and stretched our legs. We were hoping Fair Grove would be like the last two towns, and if we were stupidly lucky, Springfield would have a decent sized population that we might be able to get some recruits from. I didn't have high hopes for the last, but these days you never knew.

As I got out of the van, a cold wind blew right in my face. It reminded me we weren't all that far south, but if we could get cold without snow for a while, then we could make some serious progress. We might even be able to tackle Kansas City head on and just go on a slow zombie killing spree.

Fair Grove was an interesting, sprawling community. It spread out in every direction, but it wasn't heavily populated. Off in the distance I could see a house here, a farm there, a business over there. Tommy had parked us at a bank, and there was a small strip mall next to us, but two hundred yards away was a Dollar General sitting by itself.

After looking around, I said we needed to find someone to talk to, and we'd wear our legs off trying to find someone within a mile of where we were. I didn't think anyone was dead here, but they were just far apart.

As we walked back to the van, I hung back with Charlie until Tommy and Duncan got back in the vehicle. When they were out of earshot, I whispered at Charlie.

"When are you going to tell them that your first wife and child actually died in Springfield, Illinois?"

Charlie shrugged. "Not sure. But I think after all the crap I take from those two I deserve to milk this for all its worth, don't you?"

I shook my head. "You're on your own with this one."

We got back in the van and drove towards what looked like a promising collection of buildings. There was a truck mechanic shop, a clinic, a bait shop, and some low building that we couldn't identify. A quick search showed no one was at any of the buildings.

"Okay, which way?" Tommy asked.

"Try south. We wanted to go that way anyway," I suggested.

"All righty," Tommy said. Duncan buried himself in a couple of maps.

Tommy took the van in that direction, and we quickly reached the southern end of town. There we were greeted by a curious sight.

Hundreds of people were working feverishly erecting barricades and digging trenches. Three watchtowers were fully manned, and I could see several sniper stations out in the grassy areas to the south. All of them had clear fields of fire out to five hundred yards.

I gave Charlie an approving nod. "These people have faced the fire before. But why are they preparing for it again?"

"Let's find out." Charlie stepped out of the van and walked over to a man who was directing several people to move some hay bales into a more funneling design.

"Excuse me, could you tell me…"

Charlie never got to finish his sentence before the man barked at him.

"Christ! What the hell are you idiots doing here? Report up to the front line before it's too late! What the hell? The call went out yesterday! Move!" With that, the man turned back to berating the people moving the hay bales.

Charlie turned back to me, and I shrugged.

"Guess we head south, and see what's going on," I said.

"Kind of glad the army is coming up soon," Duncan said. "Do you think it's a horde on its way? Maybe 'the' horde?"

Tommy snorted. "That's just a rumor. There's been reports for months about a huge horde that just wanders around and swallows up whole communities. Don't you think we've had found it by now?"

Duncan was unswayed. "We've been on the east side of the river. Now we are in its territory."

"Well, the good news is I have a plan should the mighty horde find us here," I said loftily.

"Would that plan involve running for the nearest high ground?" Charlie asked.

"When did I tell you my plan?"

We got back into the van and went south again. We passed another group of people digging out an old trench, and others were rebuilding old barricades. Something was seriously up. This time of year people were generally getting ready for winter and not really worrying about zombie attacks. They slowed down considerably in cold weather, even the fast ones, and one man could handle a good sized horde if he had the right weapon and was smart enough not to get completely surrounded or surprised.

We drove south for a few miles and reached a small gathering of vehicles and people. They seemed to be clustered around a small barn, but from where we were we couldn't see much else.

"Pull up back here," I said. "We don't know for sure what's going on, but clearly there is a zombie threat that is imminent."

"Full gear?" Charlie asked.

I nodded. "Packs, too."

We took a moment to get our gear on, checking our mags to make sure they were full. I had my pick and my bowie, my Glock and my rifle, and a pack full of useful goodies. I slipped my gloves on and put my balaclava on my head. I didn't pull it down over my face, though. No need for that just yet.

Tommy gave me a look, and I just shrugged. But he pulled his own out and wore it like a cap as well.

"It *is* getting colder," he said.

We stepped out and walked over to the collection of people. They were in a semi circle around a woman who appeared to be talking on an old wired phone like something from an army surplus store. She was about my age, with short black hair and wire rimmed glasses. She was wearing a simple wool coat, but I could see the bulge of a handgun where the shoulder harness she wore rode up on the left side.

"Who are you?" A voice at my left distracted me before I could talk to the woman.

The speaker was a short man, about fifty years old, and looked to be as hard as the rock he was standing on. His thick arms held a long pole that was topped with heavy chunks of jagged steel. No matter how he swung that thing, it was going to kill something. His face was a mass of black beard that was streaked with grey, and I could see dark scars down the side of his neck. Three of them equal distant apart, like a hand that had clawed at him.

I held out my hand. "John Talon. My friends here are Charlie James, Duncan Fries, and Tommy Carter. What's going on? Can we help?"

The man took my hand in a very strong grip. "Brian Wright. Pleasure. If you boys want to help, and by the look of you, you surely can, then I'll get you up front to talk to Meggie right now. Follow me."

Wright worked his way through the crowd and up to the woman. I could hear her end of the conversation, and it didn't sound good.

"You don't understand! We had a hard growth season this year, and there isn't any extra! As it is, we will probably have to forage this winter just so we can keep ourselves fed!" Meggie was clearly agitated. "If you set them loose we'll be finished, and so will your food supply forever! Have you thought about that?"

Meggie looked over at me and my companions. Her eyes got a little wide at our war-readiness, but she recovered quickly enough to answer to whoever she was speaking to.

"I'm not holding anything back. But I will say this. If you turn them loose, our agreement is over. And if we survive the attack, it will be open season on you and your gang, do you understand me?" Meggie surely had had enough of the conversation, but then she looked at me as she listened to the phone.

"I have no idea. They just showed up. They don't live around here. What? Why do you...? No! I didn't hire them! You're crazy! I've never seen them before!" Meggie was suddenly defensive.

I turned to my crew. "Someone has eyes on us. I want eyes on them."

"You got it," Charlie said. The three of them left the group to find covered places to start scanning for threats.

I turned back to Meggie who was looking at me again.

"I don't know what he just did or why those men left. What? Fine. Hold on." Meggie held the phone out to me. "It's for you."

I took the phone. "Hi. I'm John, by the way."

"Meggie. Nice to meet you. If you and your men can get us out of this I will be very grateful," she said, running a hand over her eyes.

I spoke into the old phone. It was a relic from the past, and I wondered briefly why they didn't use CB radios or something, but it didn't really matter.

"This is John, who am I talking to?" I asked, trying to speak loudly enough so the people around me could hear the conversation.

"Listen, asshole. You'd better take your little band and get the fuck out of here. I don't know who you are or what you are about, but this is my fucking deal, and those people fucking owe me and my crew my supplies, understand?" The voice on the other end of the line was agitated and slightly high pitched with a nasal undertone that was thoroughly annoying. I remembered another person with a voice like that, and he was annoying as well. He died in a pit of zombie heads, as I recall.

"No, I actually don't understand. Wait, hold on." I put the phone down to listen to my radio.

"John? This is Tommy, over."

"Go ahead, over."

"I got them. About five hundred yards south, sitting near that old farmhouse with the caved in widow's walk. Over."

I glanced up and saw where he was looking. Not an easy shot, but Tommy could do it. Charlie could as well. Duncan might hit the house, he might not.

"Take the shot? Over."

"Not yet. I get the feeling there's more of these jerks out there. Over."

"Roger that. Over." Charlie's voice came through the radio five by five.

I picked the phone up again.

"Sorry about that. Had to talk to my guys briefly," I said, winking at Meggie.

The voice on the phone was not very understanding. "Fuck your sorry, and fuck you. You know what I'm going to do? I'm going to let loose about a thousand zombies right now right up your ass, you hear me? That fucking town is dead and everyone in it, you get that asshole? This is on you." The voice had taken on more of that nasal tone, and it wasn't fun to listen to.

"If you say so. But you might want to reconsider that," I said, raising my hand.

"Oh, are you going to threaten me now, cocksucker? Fuck you. You got gear, good for you. I don't...*Jesus!*" The voice went silent for a minute.

While he was in the middle of his tirade, I had signaled to Tommy to shoot, but to miss very closely. He must have done his job very well. The echo of the report of the rifle echoed off the low hills that spread out in every direction.

Meggie, Brian, and the rest of the group had jumped at the sound of the shot and then looked worried. I held up a reassuring hand.

"You still there?" I asked. "My man didn't kill you, did he? If he did, I'm sorry." I waited and after a minute I got a response.

"You're fucking dead. That whole town is fucking dead. You hear me? I'm turning loose every zombie in this fucking city, and I'm pointing them north. I'll—"

"Shut up, stupid," I said "I've had enough of your talk. You want to turn the spigot on, go for it. My crew and I are headed your way right now. You might make it to safety, or you might not. But you know we can shoot so you'd better be staying out of sight. As for your zombies, I have six thousand seasoned fighters on their way here right now. We could use the exercise. Set them loose. I guarantee they will eat your ass for breakfast," I said before hanging up.

I turned to see the entire group of people staring at me.

"I wasn't kidding. You will be safe. Go see to your defenses. My crew and I are going to see what we can do before the army arrives," I said.

"Who are you?" Brian asked, his eyes wide.

"John Talon, like I said. Chief Executive and Commander in Chief of the army of the New United States," I said, feeling like a pompous ass even as I said it. "We could use some representation at the new capital from Missouri," I said. "Once we clean up here, you're welcome to go up north to see what's up."

Meggie looked at me with different eyes. "You don't say. How many do you have in your 'new' capital' if you don't mind my asking?"

"About fifteen thousand, give or take a few. We've had a cold couple of winters, and the population might have expanded a little more than normal. I'll answer your questions more in a bit, but right now, time is of the essence. I have a jackass to deal with," I said, moving away from the group and starting towards our van.

I stopped suddenly and voiced a question.

"Out of curiosity, does my little nemesis have a name?" I asked.

Meggie snorted in a most unladylike way. "Him? That jerk calls himself Zim."

"Zim?"

"Yeah, it's 'Z'-'M'. Short for Zombie Master."

"I had to ask. Thank you," I said, turning back to the van where the rest of my crew was waiting for me. As I walked up, I winked at Tommy.

"Nice shot. Let's get moving. We may be cutting this one close," I said, getting inside.

"On our way south?" Tommy asked, putting the van in gear.

"Yep. Charlie, you're up top, shoot on sight. We need to stop this fool before he gets to his zombies. If we're lucky, we can get him and take advantage of whatever he's used to bottle up the Z's. If they're just sitting there en masse, then Duncan, you're up," I said.

Duncan smiled so wide I could see it from the back of his head.

As we drove south on Highway 65, I was trying to figure out how someone could control the zombies in such a way that he could just let out a few or let out a bunch? That seemed completely contrary to everything we knew about the zombies so far.

We got past a small river, and suddenly Charlie's rifle was barking. Tommy gunned the engine and raced ahead. I watched Charlie turn in the skylight and fire behind us. Tommy turned down a side street, which was East State Highway C, and came to a stop. There was a berm of dirt that almost came to the top of the van on either side of the road, and Charlie ducked back inside as several shots whined overhead.

"They were waiting for us under the bridge by the Little Sac River. I just happened to see the front end of their truck. I tried to put a few in the radiator, but I think I shot out their headlights," Charlie said.

"Hey, we're ahead of them, and we know where they are. Let's finish this idiot," I said.

"Are we sure we want to kill him? He might be useful in flushing out his partners, if he has any," Charlie said, stepping out of the van and moving over to the berm.

"He calls himself Zim," I said.

"Zim?" Asked Duncan.

"It's the letters z and m," I said. "Stands for Zombie Master."

Tommy and Duncan spoke at the same time.

"Kill him."

I joined Charlie at the berm, and together we swung our rifles back and forth, looking for the guy who shot at us. If I had bothered to reason it out, I guess we could have been in the wrong since we did shoot first. He did threaten everyone within a twenty mile radius with death and zombification, so I felt a lot less bad than perhaps I might have.

"Nothing on this side; do you think he booked it from the truck?" Charlie asked.

"No place really to go unless he had a side route he followed," I said, scanning my side. I wasn't looking for anything that was standing still; I figured this guy had to be moving and moving fast. He was far away from his source of power, and if we could keep it that way, we'd be in good shape.

"Tommy!" I called out.

"What?"

"Take the van and Duncan and get to the city. Find out what's up and what we can do about it. See if this guy is alone or not," I said.

"If he isn't?" Tommy asked.

"Do what you need to do," I said. "This bunch seems to have held this area hostage, so I'm not inclined to be charitable. "

"Hey Duncan!" Charlie called.

"Yes?"

"Try not to let the zombies out if you can help it."

"Only for you."

Charlie turned back to me.

"You figure if he sees the van drive off towards his city he'll break cover and chase it?" he asked, scanning the area with his scope again.

"That was the plan," I said, trying to see through trees and brush anything that might hide a vehicle.

"Not bad. Let's see if he takes the bait. The last shots came from over there, and we haven't heard any since, so he must have moved around us, or he's sitting tight, hoping we go away," Charlie said.

I scanned the trees by the lake and the creek and didn't see anything. I looked behind me and watched our van get smaller and smaller. I was starting to think I had made a mistake when Charlie tapped me on the arm.

"Here he comes."

A dark green pickup truck slowly emerged from the small copse of trees in front of us. It was moving slow, like it had a problem with its engine. As it got closer, I could see the driver, a young man of about twenty or so. He was keeping his speed about forty miles an hour, and I could see in my scope that he was extremely impatient. He kept shaking the wheel and slamming his hands on the console.

Charlie chuckled.

"Guess I hit him after all," he said.

"How do you know?" I asked.

"He'd be driving faster if he could," Charlie explained. "You can drive your car up to forty miles an hour for about fifteen minutes when you don't have any anti-freeze. After that you'd better find a place for lunch because you're not going anywhere."

"When do you want to take him?" I asked, watching the truck get closer.

"I'd say we let him pass, then take the tires out. Should be an easy shot from behind," Charlie said.

We ducked down and waited, keeping ourselves out of sight. At that speed, he'd see us for sure, if he hadn't already. I asked Charlie what he planned to do if the truck stopped in front of us and Zim started shooting. We were pretty well exposed out here on the road.

Charlie shrugged. "I guess if he stops, we open up on him first and get to cover behind these hills."

I was good with that.

The truck wheezed its way towards us, and we were forced to wait a lot longer than I thought we needed to. But then I remembered that scopes on rifles made things seem closer than they really were, and the truck was a lot further away than it really was. Experience taught me not to mention this thought to Charlie while we waited.

Charlie took a peek over the nearest hill, and gave me the signal to get flat on the hill closest to the truck. A casual glance would pass us by, but a good look would find us quickly. I was hoping Zim would be more focused on getting to his pet hordes than looking for enemies.

After a minute in the grass, the truck ran past. I don't think the driver gave the side road a glance at all. Charlie sprang off the ground and practically leaped to the top of the hill on the other side of the road. I wasn't as graceful, but I got there a second after he did.

Looking through my scope, I saw the lovely rear left tire in intimate detail as it rolled along the road. I was sure Charlie saw the same thing, only on the right side.

"Ready? Three, two, one, now," I said, squeezing off my shot the same time Charlie did.

The rear tires blew out immediately, and the truck lurched back on its haunches as the rear end dropped to the ground. The brake lights shone brightly as the driver slewed the vehicle first one way and then the other. Finally it stopped in the middle of the road, and the man known as Zim popped out of the truck like he had a spring in his ass and started sprinting towards the south.

Charlie and I fired again, putting a bullet on either side of his running feet. He got the message clearly, and stopped, putting his hands in the air. We came down the hill, and I walked around to the front of our extortionist to see what it was we were dealing with.

Zim proved to be different than I thought. I expected to see some sort of nasty, pasty-faced loser who probably had no friends in the world before the zombies. What I got was a young man of about twenty-five, with model good looks, and piercing dark eyes.

"Well, Zim, it seems like your plan of unleashing a horde of zombies on me just came to a crashing halt," I said, casually aiming my rifle at his chest while Charlie tied his hands with a zip tie.

"I still have friends. When they see I'm not back, they'll let the whole horde loose. You'll see. Whatever is left of the population around here is toast," Zim said.

"Does it bother you that you'll be part of the toast?" I asked.

"Fuck you. What are you gonna do now? Kill me? Go for it. The zombies get out. Put me in jail? Fuck you, the zombies get out. Face it, jackass. Even as a captive I have more power than you," Zim snarled.

I had to admit, he had a point, and as much as I wanted to just shoot him or leave him out for the zombies to eat, I had to figure out a way to contain the threat.

"Let's walk, asshole," I said, gesturing with the barrel of my rifle.

"If I refuse? Same rules, jackass," Zim smirked.

His smirk lasted a second, and then it was replaced with a look of shock as Charlie brought his fist crashing into the side of Zim's head. Zim went down like the proverbial sack of crap. He didn't get to lay there; Charlie grabbed him by the shoulders and lifted him back on his feet. Zim's eyes were glazed over for a moment before he recovered and figured out what had just happened.

"Ow! Motherfucker! You can't…wait!" Zim's sentence was cut off as Charlie hit him again, let him fall, then put him back on his feet.

It took a little while longer for the effect to wear off. I had a little sympathy for him. I'd been hit by Charlie before in training, and it always felt like getting hit with a sack full of rocks.

This time Charlie spoke. "These are the rules, jackass. You open your stupid mouth to be insulting, and I will punch you to the ground. If you do not learn this rule, I will beat you half to death. If you insist on being a nasty little prick for the rest of your short life, I will finish the job I started." Charlie grabbed Zim by his long blonde hair. "Do you understand?"

Fortunately, Zim was a quick study of human behavior, and he must have concluded that the next few minutes of his life depended entirely on his ability to control his natural, albeit misplaced and potentially deadly, character flaws.

We marched Zim back the way we had come since it was a shorter walk to Fair Grove than it was to Springfield. He didn't have much to say, but I could see he clearly was not liking the fact that we were bringing him back to the place that he had exploited for so long.

A half hour's hike brought us to the small shed and the table where the original phone conversation had taken place. The people of Fair Grove were finished with their preparations, and when we arrived a small group came out to meet us. Meggie was with them, as was Brian.

"Here's Zim. He's not so scary once you knock some sense into him," Charlie said.

Zim glared bloody murder at Charlie, but he should have been paying better attention. Brian came up and slammed a fist in Zim's gut, folding him in half, and dropping him to the ground.

Brian raised a hand to strike again, but I held up a hand. "There's been enough of that, thanks."

Brian snorted. "I don't take orders from you." He raised his fist again, and I stuck the barrel of my rifle in his face.

"Now you will. Hit him again, and I will see how many of your teeth I can blow out the back of your head. I figure I'll be protecting someone from murder." I must have had a serious enough look on my face because Brian backed off.

Meggie came to the rescue by pulling Brian off. "Thank you, Mr. Talon. I appreciate your help. What has become of your other crew members?" She looked past my shoulder, but I doubted she would be able to see where Tommy and Duncan were.

"They went to see if the zombies were really contained and whether or not Zombie Master here was actually working alone," I said. If we could borrow some kind of vehicle, any kind, I'd be grateful."

Meggie nodded and waved a hand to another man who ran off towards the town. "What do we do with him?" Meggie asked, more out loud to her people than to me.

"String him up! Don't waste a bullet on him!"

"Kill him!" My daughter almost starved last winter!"

"Feed him to the zombies!"

Meggie gave me a half smile and then turned it on Zim. "I guess the people have spoken, Mr. Zim. Get him up, find a rope, and a tree."

"I think not," Charlie said, unslinging his rifle from his shoulder.

"What? What do you mean?" Meggie turned to me. "This man has extorted us for the last two years, threatening to send zombies to us if we didn't pay his demands. He deserves to pay for that!"

"I agree with you a hundred percent, Meggie, I really do. But while he's a loud mouth asshole, I have to give him credit for keeping the scam going this long. Have any of you actually been near Springfield?" I asked. I didn't get any responses to my question. "Did any of you ever actually ask yourself how he managed to keep thousands of zombies in check?"

Still no answer.

"Since he never really let any zombies loose, I for one can't really say whether or not there are actually any zombies held in captivity. Bottom line is this. You aren't going to kill him because all he did was make you look stupid for believing his bullshit," Charlie said. "I hit him because he was an ass, that's all."

"If I were you, I'd drive him fifty miles away in any direction and dump him off with a warning he'd be shot on sight if he ever dared to show his face around these parts again," I said.

Brian glared at me. "I ain't you. And I won't be forgetting you put a gun in my face."

I looked back at Brian. "It might be better if you do." I looked over at Meggie. "We'll take that ride now. I leave this matter in your hands, "I said. "But don't kill him."

Meggie looked down at Zim and then at the people gathering. "And if we do?"

"Then we will have a serious problem. Let's not let it get there," I said. I turned to Charlie. "Let's go see what we have down south. We're done here," I said. I turned to look at Meggie and Brian. "For now."

We travelled south in a very beat up Monte Carlo that was nearly older than I was. The damn thing had a hole in the floorboards that let in fumes from the exhaust pipe which also had a hole. Charlie and I spent a very uncomfortable ride down the road, with both of us sticking our heads out of the car windows like a couple of dogs enjoying rare car trip.

When we were about a mile from the city, I got a call over the radio.

"John, is that you in the blue car heading south? Over."

It was Duncan. "That's us, we'll be there in a few minutes. Over."

"Okay. What are you guys carrying? It looks like you have a rug sticking out of the front windows. Over."

I looked over at Charlie. "Never mind. Over."

Charlie smiled. "You do need a haircut."

"Shut up."

We reached the outlying areas of Springfield and began to notice that the cars on the roads were all tipped onto their sides. As we looked closer, we saw that there was movement in between the cars. I scanned the cars with my rifle scope, and the first look I got was a grey ghoul's face looking right back at me. By reflex, I very nearly pulled the trigger.

I got on the radio. "Duncan, we're here, over. Where are you? Over."

"We see you. We'll be right there. Over," Duncan said.

In a minute the van came up from the west and pulled alongside the Monte Carlo. I was very glad any more travel was going to happen in a vehicle that didn't require a gas mask.

"So what's the story?" Charlie asked. "We caught the Zombie Master and turned him in to the people of Fair Grove."

"Ah, hell," Duncan said. "There's a problem with that."

"I'm going to hope you aren't like Tommy, and you will just tell the story in one shot and not drag it out," I said.

"It will be short. We caught up to the people who were keeping the zombies in their pens. They told us a very different story. Turns out Zim had been contracted by the people of Fair Grove to do something about the constant threat of Zombies from the bigger town. So Zim and his crew figured out a way to keep the zombies contained in these pens of cars. They lost two people trying it, but in the end it worked out. Trouble was, the good people of Fair Grove didn't want to pay what they owed."

I interrupted. "Now it makes sense when he said they owed him and his crew."

"Exactly, so we need to get back and keep them from killing that guy, despite his stupid nickname," Tommy said.

"Shit, let's move," I said, getting into the van.

As we drove back, I began to think about the preparations we had seen, especially the sniper towers. I hoped we weren't going to be waging a losing battle from five hundred yards away.

As it turned out, I needn't have worried. A literal sea of trucks, trailers, and other vehicles were scattered all over the road and stretched back for miles. About two hundred fighters were in a semi-circle around the small group we had left earlier, and about twenty of them were keeping their rifles pointed at the smaller group. I could see a short, dark-haired woman keeping things under control at the center of the standoff.

We pulled up, and I immediately got out, walking over to the group. I was glad things had not gotten out of control yet, but I was pissed that the town had duped me.

I went over to Sarah and gave her a quick hug as thanks for keeping things under control. She smiled, and I nodded to two unit leaders who gave a hand signal to their troops. Immediately the rifles that were pointed at the townspeople were aimed in a more safe direction.

Brian was there, as was Meggie. I directed my comments towards them.

"So. You made a deal, and when it went your way, you tried to keep from holding up your end of the bargain, yes?" I asked quietly. "And then you let us think that Zim was the bad guy."

I went over to Zim who was standing by three of my fighters. He looked very relieved, yet mad at the same time. I didn't blame him, he'd been treated badly all around.

"My apologies for my comrades' actions and for mine. We acted in haste, and we should have taken the time to get your story," I said.

Charlie nodded. "Sorry for roughing you up there."

Zim was more calm now that things seemed to have gone his way. "Just glad your friends showed up. They were going to kill me." He pointed at Brian and Meggie.

"Looks like you and your friends down at Springfield need to relocate, "I said. There's a lot of good places across the river if you're interested in a change of scenery."

"Thanks. Let me get back to them and talk to them," Zim said.

Zim rode off on a small motorcycle, and I turned back to Meggie and Brian.

"Don't send anyone from your town to represent this area. We don't want your kind up in the new capital."

Maggie glared, but Brian spoke up.

"You ain't the boss here. We didn't elect you. So why don't you take your army and fuck off?" he snarled.

"Presently, presently," I said. "We are moving on, and you are on your own. You'll figure out what that means in a few years, but for now, I think I'll just leave it up to your imagination."

I waved my hand in a circular motion, and the fighters went back to their vehicles. There was a loud roar as hundreds of vehicles started up.

"Son of a bitch!" Brian leapt to his feet and lunged at me, his huge fists swinging.

I dodged to the side and slammed an elbow into the side of his head, knocking him sideways and down. I raised a hand to keep my fighters back while Brian regained his feet. He spat a glob of blood out of his mouth, and I didn't wait for him to get set. Moving forward suddenly, I snapped a jab to his mouth and followed it with a fist to his gut. Brian's eyes got wide as his breath left him, and I slammed another elbow to his head. This time he went down, and it took a little longer for him to get up.

"I admire your sand, Mr. Wright, but I would hope you'd reconsider before this gets serious. Right now we've had a bit of a disagreement, but I hope we don't get into a full blown argument," I said, stepping away as he reached out with a clumsy hand to try and grab my leg.

Brian apparently hadn't learned when he was outclassed, and came off his feet with a lunge, he arms wide to try and pull me in close where his strength would be of an advantage for him.

Unfortunately for him, this was a move we taught all of our fighters, since many times zombies will come off the ground with their arms out in an attempt to grab whatever they can reach and pull it in for a bite. Best way to deal with it was to lean to the side and direct the attack away from you which is what I did with Brian. He went sideways and fell on his face again, and I waited for him to get up.

"I'm done with this, Mr. Wright. And so are you. If this keeps up I'll have to kill you, and I'd rather not do that. Would you be so kind as to give up?" I asked.

Brian spat again, then abruptly turned on his heel and stormed off. I watched him go for a moment then turned back to Sarah.

"Good timing," I said, giving her another hug.

"Yeah, we pulled in here and things seemed just a whole lot weird. Once we saw this group about to hang the young man over there, I figured we needed to do something about it. What did he do, by the way?" Sarah asked.

"Kept the town from being overrun by zombies," I said.

I didn't elaborate just because the look on Sarah's face was priceless.

We backed the semi trucks up to one of the barricades that Zim had built out of cars. We learned that he had originally been contacted by the people of Fair Grove to build a barricade for them around their town. Zim had been a large fork truck operator back in the old days and used his skills to start moving cars around. The zombies were attracted to the noise, and he soon started penning in the ghouls to keep them out of his way. After a while he had realized he'd turned the zombie population of Springfield, Missouri into prisoners. When he tried to collect from the town, they crawfished on the deal. That's where we came into the picture.

It took three days of work, but in the end we managed to wipe out the population of Springfield. The corpses burned for two days, and we spent that time relaxing, gathering supplies, and making plans for the next part of the war. Winter was coming on, and there were cities I wanted to take.

MONTANA

"So he headed east, did he? And locked you up in a guard shack." Cole looked at his son with no small measure of disgust. "And now he's gone, and we really don't know which way to go to catch him and bring him back."

Cole stood up from the table and turned his back on the two men seated there. *God, things were simple once. Get up in the morning, get your chores done, and head home of an evening*, he thought. *Now it's a bunch of complaints and problems, and now we have stories of an army spinning around. Great. Just great.*

Cole turned back to the men. "Is there anyone we can send out to try and find him? What about your trackers? They've found men before."

Luke Blacktail nodded. "They ought to. They're full-blooded Ogallala. Came up from the reservation outside of Cheyenne when Denver fell and the ghouls headed north.

"Are they willing to go after Tibbles?"

"Right now, they are not exactly motivated. The first snows have fallen, and more is coming. They get caught up there in the mountains, they're dead men, and they know it. Darnell was not stupid, and he timed his run nearly perfectly. Anyone you send after him will likely not come back before spring which will turn off most men," Luke said.

Carson spoke up. "We could just order them to go. Why are we wasting time talking about it?"

Luke looked over at the young man. "Because that would prove Darnell was right, and the last thing your father needs right now is open rebellion when winter is coming."

Cole looked at his son. "Shut up until I ask you a question. You've proven you can't handle an older man and a young girl. I ought to let you try to order the Sioux around and watch them laugh in your face."

Carson looked down, his face turning red. He had screwed up, but the man had a gun! Was he supposed to die for this shithole?

Cole Hobbes took a deep breath and let it out slowly. "Okay, here's what we'll do. Darnell is gone, over the fence and into zombie territory. He survives, good for him, he'll never come back anyway. Story over. No point in chasing him and risking anyone's life."

"What about the army?" Luke asked.

Cole nodded. "I'm a little curious about those myself. Did you get any more information from that scout that made it back?"

"Nothing of substance. The man had just travelled a couple thousand miles by himself," Luke said. "But I can send out two more if you want. An army of any size would be noticed from a long way off. If they leave today, they should get through the passes before the snow comes, and with the cold coming on, the zombie threat is less."

Cole slapped his heavy hand on the hardwood table. "That's the plan, then. Pick your men, then get them gone. They have thirty days. I want them back before the end of the year."

Blacktail rose and then stopped. "What if we get a winter like we did a year ago? The snow almost filed the canyon."

"We'll keep a passage open," Cole said, as he turned to his son. "That's your job. Find a couple of friends that owe you a favor. You're camping over the wall for the next thirty days."

Carson scowled but kept his thought to himself. He'd tried bucking his dad before, and it took the intervention of Heather Hobbes to keep Cole from seriously injuring his son.

Darnell was cold. He didn't tell his daughter because she would worry, but he was deep down chilled to the bone cold. They slept during the day and walked at night, the reasoning being that the sun would keep them warmer as they recovered from their previous walk. It was more dangerous to travel at night, but Darnell was hopeful they would reach the Spring Creek road before the next sunrise. From there, they could move from campground to campground, heading south along a much easier path. Right now they had just walked until they reached the foot of the mountain, then followed the valleys. Sometimes they had to go in directions they didn't want to, but overall they made good progress.

Alison was leading the way since she had better eyes and could see further in the dark. Darnell just concentrated on stepping where she stepped and keeping out of the way.

Suddenly, Alison stopped. "Dad!" she whispered quietly, but urgently.

Darnell's head snapped up. He looked around and saw several shadowy figures moving slowly in the open grass next to a noisy creek. A quick head count told him there were more of them than bullets in his gun. Not a great place to be, mathematically.

"Don't move," Darnell said. "We're in a good spot here. They can't see us in the trees, and they can't hear us with the creek nearby. "There's no wind, so they can't smell us. Just be patient, and let them pass."

Alison was frozen with fear. "But what if they hear us or know we're here?" Her voice started to rise above a whisper, and Darnell put a kind hand on his daughter's mouth.

"Then we run for the nearest mountain and go up. It's too cold for them to follow, and they're moving slow as it is. Pretty soon they're going to be frozen," Darnell said with more confidence than he felt. Deep down he was terrified as the small horde of about a dozen zombies slowly made their way towards him and his daughter.

They moved very slowly, and it was strange to watch them walk nearly in unison. But they made their way slowly towards the small grove of trees that hid the terrified pair. Occasionally one would turn its head and smell the air with a large intake of air. But they always moved on, pushing aside long grass and sometimes tripping over hidden rocks.

Darnell turned his daughter to face him. "Sit down by the big tree there. I'll sit over at this one. Don't move unless you have to. And if you have to, head to your right, and make a run for the mountain. It's our only chance," Darnell said, as he saw the question in Alison's eyes. She nodded and silently sat down on the side of the tree away from the zombies. Darnell ducked down and made it over to the other tree facing the same way. No moans behind him suggested that they had gotten away with their little bit of movement. It was very dark, and the only way Alison had seen the zombies in the first place was one of them had glowing eyes.

Darnell used his hands and told his daughter to cover her head with her hood and keep her face down. He'd had to do this before when he was running from the zombies during the first days of the Upheaval. He'd been chased down an alleyway by three of them, and around the corner was a car covered in a tarp. He'd slipped under the tarp when they couldn't see him, and they walked right on by. He hoped it was a pattern, and he didn't just kill himself and his daughter.

He put his own head down, and with his eyes closed he listened as the footsteps got closer and closer. They were about fifteen feet away, then ten, then five. The next sounds were the zombies walking around them, slowly, shifting through the grass, stumbling over the rocks.

From under his hood, Darnell could see a foot stepping inches away from his own foot, just fuzzy blurs in the darkness, but Darnell could sense the ghoul beside him. He was grateful it was cold, but he could feel a line of sweat starting at the back of his neck and running down his back. His own heart was beating so loud he was amazed the zombies couldn't hear it. He didn't dare move to see how Alison was doing, but he hoped she was still and quiet. He'd know otherwise.

It took forever, but eventually the sounds faded away, and Darnell still counted to two hundred before he slowly, slowly lifted his head and scanned the area from underneath his hood. He looked around from side to side, then slowly he stood up, stretching legs that were suddenly screaming with cramps. He turned around and very slowly looked around the tree, making sure there were no stragglers. He'd seen it before. Some family dodged a horde, only to fall right into the next one that was just behind the first.

Darnell stepped over to his daughter and put a hand on her shoulder. She jumped slightly, and he could feel her shaking under her hood.

"Let's go, honey," he whispered, barely above the sound of normal breath.

Alison grabbed her father's hand and pointed with the other one. In the brush, crawling very slowly, was another zombie. It was staring at Alison with greedy, glowing eyes, struggling to get closer as it opened and closed its mouth in anticipation.

Darnell felt a sudden fear, but he pulled his daughter up, and holding her hand, led her around the tree and away from the small horde and the thing in the grass. As he walked he shook his head, thinking about how hard it must have been for Alison to see that thing getting closer and closer and not being able to scream or move because the other zombies would surely have killed them both.

They moved quietly away, keeping low and trying to stay near rocks and other obstacles that would keep the crawling monsters away. Darnell decided it would be better to travel a little higher up the mountain where it would be easier to evade any zombies, but Alison voted him down, saying they could move a lot faster in the valleys, even though it was more dangerous. The cold weather was the deciding factor, as even chillier winds blew down from the peaks.

"We're going to need shelter soon," Darnell said. He was even colder than before, since the sweat from the last zombie encounter was starting to chill him.

Alison nodded. She kept moving ahead, working her way around rocks and deadfalls. She moved quickly but quietly, trying to put as much distance as she could between her and the last batch of zombies.

The moon suddenly came out between the clouds and the valley was suddenly bathed in pale light. Alison didn't miss a beat. She froze in place, just as her father did, and the two of them slowly checked the terrain for anything that might be deadly before moving on.

The road appeared suddenly, without any warning whatsoever. One minute Darnell was dragging his feet through some tenacious grass, and the next minute he was stumbling into the back of his daughter because his feet were suddenly free.

Alison turned abruptly and grabbed her father, hugging him closely. She'd been so close to getting bit, and to have escaped like that at the last minute was almost more than her seventeen-year-old mind could handle. Even though she had survived the journey to Montana, right now she needed her dad.

"Whoa, girl! I got you, I got you," Darnell said, holding his daughter while she worked to get the shakes out of her system. He had to give her credit, she didn't lose it when that thing in the grass was coming for her. If she had made even a sound they'd have been slaughtered.

Darnell made sure she understood that. He took her face in his hands and looked into her eyes. "Sweetheart, that was the bravest thing I had ever seen. You held it together when it mattered the most, and you saved us both. Do you understand that? You saved us both." Darnell looked at the road. "And you got us to this road. Do you know what that means?"

Alison shook her head, her eyes gleaming with unspent tears.

"We made it. We got away. Now all we have to do is get out of the mountains before snowfall, find a place to spend the winter, and we can start over," Darnell said.

Alison smiled, even though she knew her father was just trying to make her feel better. They had very little chance of getting out of the mountains before snow blocked the passes and roads, and they were on foot. Where would they go? They were alone in a sea of zombies, and no one was coming to save them.

"Come on," Darnell said. "Let's get moving down the road. If I remember right, there should be campsites along this road. We can spend the day in one and get some real rest." Tibbles was really feeling his age and the cold, and hoped the nearest one wasn't too far away.

"What if the zombies are there?" Alison said.

Darnell shrugged. "Right now, I'd fight a hundred of the damn things to get some decent rest."

The pair moved steadily down the road. It was an old logging road which the state had taken over and maintained as an access road into the mountains for fighting fires and conducting forestry surveys. The campsites were places that the firefighters would go to rest during burn season. Hikers were allowed to use the sites as well, and they were a welcome change from sleeping outside.

As they walked, they heard the sound of running water, and soon it became apparent that the road was following the river.

Darnell was amazed at his luck. If they got attacked, they had the perfect retreat right next to them.

The road was far from perfect, and three winters without maintenance had done a good bit of damage. But it was certainly better than trying to make their way through the rough country of the mountains, and with the woods on one side, a small but swift river on the other, they made ten times the progress they had made before.

A little before dawn, when the sky over the eastern ridge was changing from deep blue to a slightly lighter shade of blue, Alison pointed out the sign that hung from a tree. "Indian Hill Campground". She gave her dad's hand a little squeeze and together they walked over the small bridge that crossed the river.

The campground was mostly empty spaces under trees where people would set up tents or campers and then do their hiking or outdoor whatever. There were spaces for RV's, and a small concrete building that looked like it was for taking showers and such. A small log cabin was near where the driveway made a big circle, and behind it Darnell could see the remains of an old plastic play set.

"Let's try the cabin," Darnell said. It looked abandoned, but then it was the middle of the night, and people with any sense were asleep and safe at this time of day.

The pair walked over to the small structure, carefully walking around it and trying to see in the windows. The fact that the ground around the building was undisturbed, and there was dirt and debris piled up against the door, told Darnell that no one was at home.

The door latch was interesting; it had a doorknob as well as a lever to lift the latch to open the door. That told Darnell that there should not be any zombie in there since they would never have figured out how to open that door.

Holding the gun out in the open, Darnell pulled up the lever and then turned the doorknob. The door hinges squeaked in protest as the dirt was moved aside. Darnell walked into the small foyer and took a look around. Apart from the slight layer of dust over everything, the structure seemed to be sound and in decent shape. Darnell couldn't see any sign of activity, either from the two or four-legged kind, and that was actually a welcome relief.

The building consisted of a front room that held a desk, a small stand that held maps and flyer, and a couple of captain's chairs. In the room behind the reception area there was a small kitchenette, a bathroom, and a back room that had a cot, a tiny wood burning stove, and a small writing desk. There was a phone on the desk that Darnell was tempted to pick up, but stopped himself when he realized that even if it had a dial tone, he didn't have anyone to call.

"You take the cot, sweetheart; I'll crash in the chairs up front," Darnell said.

"Daddy, you're beat. Why don't you take the cot?" Alison argued.

"I'll be fine. I'll just push the chairs together and I've got my own cot," Darnell smiled, thinking about it. "Well, more like a bathtub, but I can at least put my feet up."

"All right, but at the next one, you take the cot," Alison said.

"Deal. Go to bed, honey." Darnell kissed his daughter on the forehead, and watched her go to the back room. She'd likely hit the cot sleeping despite the scare they both had gone through.

Darnell sat in one of the chairs up front and slid the other one close. When he put his feet up, his entire body just fell into a relaxed state, and he began to warm up. He thought about the situation and figured he could be a lot worse off. They had shelter, and pretty good protection from any zombies wandering around, as the house was made of brick and surrounded by thick bushes. The windows were all nearly six feet off the ground and were set in so they wouldn't be easy to strike at. There was water right nearby, and fish and game were close at hand. The more he thought about it, the better Darnell liked it.

As he drifted off to sleep, Darnell's thoughts wandered back to the report the scout had given. There was an army out there. But where was it? Who was in charge? And most importantly, could he turn it north?

FAYETTEVILLE, AK

"Did you know you have a zombie walk?" Sarah asked.

I shook off the bits of zombie goop that were clinging tenaciously to my pickaxe. Normally the stuff just slid off, thanks to a strange but useful discovery by Rebecca not too long ago. She found that if we sprayed WD-40 on our weapons before a fight, they didn't get as messy as when we didn't.

I stopped when it registered what Sarah had just said.

"I walk like a zombie?" I asked.

"No, silly. You have a certain way of walking when you are about to take on a Z one on one," Sarah explained.

"Do tell."

"Rebecca and I noticed it over the last few engagements."

"Don't tell me Charlie has one, too," I groaned.

"He does, and it's different than yours," Sarah said. "When Charlie goes after a zombie, he goes straight in, no subtlety, all business."

"And what do I do differently?" I asked, not being entirely sure I wanted to hear the answer.

"You tend to circle a little to either the left or right, and when you're ready, there's a burst of activity, and then there's a dead ghoul," Sarah smiled.

"And here I thought you two were just admiring our butts," I said, giving her a quick kiss.

"How do you think we began to notice you two had zombie walks?" Sarah asked sweetly.

"Could we call it something else? Like 'Zombie Stalking Technique,' or something, anything cooler than 'Zombie Walk?'" I asked.

"Nope."

"Damn."

We walked back towards the campsite that we shared with the other half of the army. We were three thousand strong and spread out in a place called Hobbs State Park. There was a huge lake in this area that twisted and turned and had branches going every which way. Duncan took one look at it and wondered why they didn't name it Centipede Lake since that's what it reminded him of. We'd been here a week, taking a break from the campaign and enjoying what seemed to be decent weather. It was just over fifty degrees, and that was a welcome change from the cold we'd had from the previous few weeks. It was late November, and we were in a decent spot to start the Killing Season in the Zombie War. I'd sent half of the army south to make a run through Louisiana, and the reports coming back were pretty positive. I hadn't heard anything from the group I had sent north, but I didn't expect to see them until we met up again on the near side of the Rockies.

"Penny for you thoughts," Sarah said, holding my side.

"A penny? Heck, my thoughts cost at least a nickel," I said.

"That's what I pay for your advice," Sarah replied, giving me a pinch.

"Ow! Alright!" I rubbed my side. "I was just thinking about this area."

"What about it?"

"It's the perfect place for a retreat from the zombies. We're surrounded by hills and water, there's actually game enough to keep us in fresh meat and fish, and there's enough level ground to raise some crops," I said.

"But there's no one here except us," Sarah said. "I see what you mean. Think there's a danger?"

I shrugged. "I'm not seeing one, but it's odd. We've hit a few zombie strongholds, but the cold weather played that one in our favor. We're missing one around here, missing something."

"Well, talk to Charlie, and see what he has to say. This used to be his back yard, and if anyone can sense what's in the wind, he can," Sarah said.

"That's usually Duncan's breath," I said. Lately Duncan had found some wild onions and had taken to chewing them. Last time he burped he killed a bug that happened to be flying by.

"Funny guy."

We reached the perimeter of the camp, and I gave a quick report to the captain of the watch. He made a note in his book about it, and we went on our way. When we reached our campsite, I was glad to see Jake outside playing with a few other boys from other fighter's families. There was a group of about six women who were sitting around a table just talking away. I slipped away from Sarah before she could snare me into a discussion and went to find Charlie.

After a good half an hour of playing "Where's Charlie?" I located the man down by the lake teaching his daughter how to hunt for turtles. It was such an innocent thing to watch that I just waited an extra ten minutes while the huge zombie killer lifted lily pads while his little girl waited with hands folded to see if there was a little reptile looking back.

I coughed discretely, and Rebecca was the first one to notice me. She smiled, and went over to Charlie who finally looked over at me. He straightened up, and after handing Julia off, he wandered over.

"What's up?"

"Got something I need to run by you; can you spare a minute?" I said.

"Sure. Come up to the trailer." Charlie led the way through the trees, and we came up to his home. It was a trailer similar to mine, but a little shorter. He didn't need the extra room since he only had one child with him.

"So what's on your mind?" Charlie asked. "Is it the creepy feeling you get because there should be more people around here, but there aren't?"

"That'd be the one," I said. "I talked to Sarah about it this morning. We went and dealt with that single sighting south of here, but there's something off about this area."

"I hear you. Place like this in Arkansas, there should be at least dozens of communities in this area," Charlie said. "On the other hand, maybe they went someplace else."

"I don't know. We've been doing this too long to believe that things just happen, usually there's a—" I was interrupted by a loud banging on the door.

A voice was urgently following the banging. "Commander James! Commander James! There's a situation, and we can't find Chief Executive Talon!" The banging continued. "Commander James, are you in there?"

I opened the door, and the young man sent to find us nearly tumbled into the trailer. I put a hand on his chest to stop his movement and gently pushed him back out the door.

He recovered quickly enough. "Sir! What a relief to find you sir. I've been looking all over for you and was told you were over this way. No one told me you were in the trailer, but that's okay, you're here, and that's what matters."

"Situation, son?" Charlie asked politely, once the linguistic tornado had subsided.

"Sir! We've lost four scouts, sir."

"Where, how? Dead?" I asked, not wanting to believe it. Our scouts were valuable members of the army, clearing the way for the larger group and avoiding any obstacles or traps. Oftentimes they had to act as ambassadors, smoothing the way for survivors to enter into the fold.

"Don't know, sir. One pair went over the hill into an area that looked like it might be occupied, and they didn't return. A second group went after them to see what had happened, and they never returned. Commander Hanley said he won't risk any more men until we figure this one out."

Smart man. This was a job for a small team or the whole army. Trouble was, with the area around us seemingly clear of zombies, the potential for a whole bunch of them nearby was possible.

"All right," Charlie said. "We'll go have a look." He looked at me. "You want to grab Duncan and Tommy for this?"

I shook my head. "We'll keep it simple. Look, learn, and leave. We'll decide if we need more men once we figure out what's going on."

We dismissed the young man, and Charlie set about getting himself together. He put on his vest, his backpack with his tomahawks sticking out on either side, and his sidearm. He put his main knife in its place on his left hip, and put two knives into the sheaths sewn into his boots. He wrapped his neck in a wide scarf and left only his eyes showing.

"Rifle?" Charlie asked.

"May as well, I'm going to stop and get mine," I said.

"AK or AR?" Charlie asked.

That was a good question. If I picked AR, then I only expected to hunt zombies. But if I picked the AK, then I had some thoughts about living targets as well. The AR was a great weapon, but the AK was a killer, pure and simple.

"AK," I said.

"All righty. Let me talk to Rebecca, and I will meet you over at your trailer," Charlie said.

I left his home and wandered over to mine. A brief conversation with Sarah left her nodding in approval for me going after the scouts. I took out the AK and that raised eyebrows.

"Expecting trouble?" she asked as I put extra magazines in my vest.

"Always. Something about this just makes little sense," I said. "Our scouts are too good to be ambushed or overwhelmed which means they must have been tricked."

"Do you think they are still alive?" Sarah said. The rest of the ladies in the group grew quiet at that.

"If they are, we'll bring them back. If they aren't, whoever killed them will regret it for a very short time," I said, meaning every word.

Sarah and the rest of the women nodded. In another world, they would not have approved, but in the one we lived in, vengeance was not taken lightly.

Charlie joined me, and together we went over to where the army's vehicles were being kept. We took a small car that was reasonably quiet. An electric car would have been great, but since they were rather difficult to keep charged, we'd stick with the gas ones.

We drove south, keeping an eye out for the vehicles our scouts usually used. The scenery was pretty much the same as what we had left, rolling hills and a lot of trees. We crossed two small creeks as we drove, and I kept on looking for any sign that they might have turned off the road or taken a different way.

The day was clear, and the high clouds off in the distance had the slight promise of rain, but it was far off. Charlie drove the vehicle with purpose, but we weren't rushing. At every intersection and driveway we slowed down to take a look to see if the other vehicles had passed this way. Nothing we had seen so far led us to believe that they had driven any other way than straight.

Suddenly Charlie slowed down. We were coming to a clearing in the roadsides, and the trees that had surrounded us were thinning out.

"What's up?" I asked, scanning around for threats and not seeing any.

"Something flashed in the air up ahead," Charlie said. "Pretty sure there's nothing up there that *should* be flashing."

"Right." I waited until Charlie backed the car up and exited the same time he did. We picked our way carefully through the trees and brush and made our way towards the edge of the trees. I couldn't see anything out of the ordinary, but then I saw a flash. There was a small grove of trees ahead of us, and the flash came from the air next to the tree.

"Saw it. Wonder what it is?" I asked.

Charlie thought about it. "Those trees are well placed to see anything coming for a long way off. Any bets there's a lookout platform up there?"

"No bet. But we can't approach it without being seen, and we left our scoped rifles at home," I said.

Charlie smiled. "Duncan laughed at me when I tucked this into my backpack, but it's worth it now." Charlie shrugged off his pack and rummaged around a little bit. He pulled out a small plastic tube about five inches long and about an inch and a half wide. Taking off one end, he slid a brass telescope out of the tube. It extended out to about a foot and had leather covering the front tube.

"Very nice," I admired. "Good picture?"

"It's actually very good. I think this might be an original and not a cheap replica." Charlie found a good tree for cover and kept the scope under a small covering of leaves. He looked through it for about a minute then handed it to me. "I can't see anything, but I'm willing to get a second opinion."

I took the scope and looked through it, keeping it under cover like Charlie did. The grove of trees leapt at me, and I could easily see the branches and leaves. I followed the base of the tree up, and looked for anything that hadn't grown there. I did see the flash again, and looking hard, saw a thin line from the tree to some place over the hill and into the forest.

I mentioned it to Charlie, and he looked through the telescope again. After a minute he put it away.

"I saw what you meant. I can only think of three things that line can be. It's either a zip line, a power line, or a communication line," Charlie said.

"Well, we won't learn anything more from here," I said. "If it were a communication line, then they may have seen our scouts and could give us a better idea of where they went. If it's a power line, why do they need power in a tree? If it's a zip line, then where does it go, and why is there an observation station up in the tree? All our answers lie over there."

"Since I didn't see anyone up there, shall we take a walk?" Charlie asked.

"No," I replied. "You can if you want to; I'm taking the car."

Charlie looked sheepish. "I actually forgot about that for a minute."

We drove over to the tree and took a quick look. There was a large ring nailed to the trunk, and a series of two by fours that went up the tree, like a kid's ladder to a tree house. At the top of a ladder was a platform with an open trapdoor on the bottom.

I looked at Charlie, and he held out a fist. I held mine out, and we counted to three. I came up with rock while he came up with scissors. He was going up the tree.

While he climbed, I scouted around, circling out from the tree. I found old horse manure, several wrappers, a few cigarette butts, and what looked like an old entrance to the nearby field. I figured it had to be some farmer's old access to the now overgrown land. I also found where a vehicle had turned in and had driven across the field. It looked as if this had happened recently.

Charlie came down a minute later. "Well, it's a zip line," he said. "It serves no other purpose."

"Where does it go?" I asked.

"Over into those trees. I tried to use the telescope, but it's nothing but leaves."

"Let's go take a look," I said.

"Take the car?" Charlie asked.

"May as well."

We drove carefully, trying to move as quietly as possible. The field was pretty flat, so we travelled well, and we eventually came to the edge of the woods. The trees were hard at work trying to reclaim the land they had lost generations ago, and as we got closer, I could see a kind of fence among the trees.

"Stop here," I said.

Charlie stopped, and we both got out. Following the fence, we made our way along until we reached a building. It was a two-story structure with several openings in the side which resembled ticket booths. A faded sign read 'Arkansas Renaissance Faire.' In front of the entrance were our two scout vehicles.

"Are you kidding me?" Charlie said.

"Apparently not," I said. "Wonder where our scouts are?"

"John. Over here," Charlie said. He was standing by the front of the vehicles.

I went over and saw four dead zombies, two males and two females. They were not as old looking as some we had seen lately, so I figured them to be locals who turned recently.

"Okay," I said. "These aren't our scouts, so that's a hopeful sign," I said.

"I guess so," Charlie said.

"Well, they all came this way, and the zip line guy isn't around, so let's see what we can see," I said, slipping my rifle off my shoulder and making sure a round was chambered.

We walked to the entrance and found the heavy doors were locked. Charlie went over to the side of the gate and climbed up, slipping over quietly. A second later, the gate opened, and I passed inside.

The interior of the fair was surprisingly well maintained. There were rows of structures and dwellings with large trees providing a decent canopy over everything. There seemed to be a town square in front of us with a fountain, several fruit trees, and a small kid park. Down to our left was a massive building which in its day was likely the admin offices for the fair. The place was easily as large as a good-sized house, rising at least three stories in the air.

As we walked further in, we saw abandoned booths that looked like they held archery ranges and knife throwing boards. "Do you think anyone lives here?" Charlie asked.

"Right now, I would say yes," I said looking around. The open lanes that wound through the trees were flanked on both sides by various shops and living quarters. It looked like the people who ran this place retreated here when the world ended and just stayed. From a tactical standpoint, they had shelter, a high fence to keep out the zombies, water, game to hunt, and land to grow food in.

We walked around an open area that looked like it was the place where crops were grown. A small lake on our left sported a bridge that led to another section of the village and a large wooden boat. The laundry lines told me someone lived there, although where they were was a mystery.

Crossing the bridge brought us to a very congested area. Buildings were pretty much on top of each other and crowded the available space. Huge trees in the middle of the lanes served at turning points for the streets.

"This is a lot different than what I expected a Renaissance fair to look like," Charlie said. "These buildings are pretty permanent. I was expecting a bunch of tents and hay bales."

"Same here. Went to one of these a while back; seemed like it was a more of an escape from reality than an actual fair," I said.

We went up a hill, and when we reached the top, we heard a noise like cheering. Looking down, we could see through the tree branches. In a clearing, we could see around two hundred people, most of them sitting in wooden stands. As we walked closer, we could see several people performing tricks and acrobatics, and on a small private pavilion, there were two people and our four scouts.

"What the hey?" Charlie asked.

"I think we can safe our rifles," I said. "I think these people are harmless."

Turns out they were. Once we made our presence known, the people who lived on the fair grounds were eager to show us their acts. I told them we would bring back a much larger crowd than the six of us, and if they wanted to bring their best out to play, we could certainly bring the audience.

Man, that did it. The crowd went nuts, and there was a general scurry for costumes and a lot of "Huzzah!s", whatever that meant. The scouts were a little embarrassed for the fuss they caused, but Charlie and I chalked it up to good community relations, and that was enough.

We went back to the front entrance, and by the time we got there nearly every house had a bunch of noise and activity. These people had lived here for two years without seeing anyone else, and at heart they were performers. So when they were offered a chance to play for a larger crowd, of course, they were excited.

The six of us walked through another row of shops and performing stages and headed for the front entrance. We were feeling pretty good about having a distraction for the army that everyone could enjoy, and we nearly walked into the horde of zombies that was waiting for us on the other side of the gate.

"Jesus!" Charlie said, whipping out his tomahawk and crushing the skull of a grey zombie that was coming around one of the cars. We didn't have time to do anything but start killing because they were instantly on us.

"Use the cars, funnel them!" I shouted, moving over to the left. I had about ten feet between the car and the fence, and two Z's were coming right for me. A quick glance over my shoulder showed me that Charlie had taken the right side, while the four scouts covered the middle which was the largest open space, being about twenty feet wide.

We didn't use our firearms as a general rule since we didn't want the report to echo out and cause more zombies to come our way. Plus, bullets were not reusable, so we had to be careful to make sure they were only in emergency situations, like the threat of being overrun. We weren't at the point of counting out rounds, and I hoped we never would be, but it was always in the back of my mind.

I faced my first one, a short male of indeterminate age. His shirt was half off his torso, and he sported a single bite on his neck. His eyes were huge, like he died surprised, and they stuck that way.

I closed his eyes with a single swing of my pick, and damned if I didn't think about Sarah's zombie walk discussion. I pushed him out of the way to slow down a faster ghoul that slid along the side of the car. She caught a back handed swing to her temple, and dropped for good by the wheel well.

The next three were going to be a challenge, and I was about to draw my pistol when one of the zombies suddenly fell to the ground. An arrow stuck out of its head, and I spared a glance upwards to the archer standing on the roof of the ticket building. He gave me a thumbs up, which I didn't return since the other two were nearly on me. I hooked the one on the left and pushed him into the one on the right, holding them both against the car with my pick. Black teeth snapped at my hand, and they missed me by inches. I pulled my knife with my left hand and stabbed the left one in the eye, killing him. The right one pushed back, and I gave him the same treatment.

I turned back to the fight, and a zombie plowed right into me. I dropped my pick and knife and pushed back, trying to keep the teeth from connecting. It was a young female, and she must have been into working out because she was unbelievably strong. My leverage was bad, and her teeth kept getting closer and closer to my neck. I didn't want to put my hands up any higher, because she'd bite those. I spun around, using the inertia to gain a little distance, and got my hand on her neck. She looked down and tried to work her teeth into my hand, but I was angry now. Another zombie was coming up, and I kicked him in the hip to get him away while I dealt with his girlfriend. I had the leverage, and I twisted again, slamming her head into the wall. Once, twice, and the third time was the charm as her head cracked. I dropped her when I felt her grip loosen and went back to my other zombies.

The one I had kicked was getting up, and another was working his way along the wall. Another arrow killed the first one, and that gave me time to get my pick and bury it in the skull of the Z by the wall.

I leaned against the wall and caught my breath. Anyone that tells you combat is easy is either a liar or has never done it. I looked over at the rest of the crew, and we were all in a state of catching our breath. Several zombies were dead by arrows, and I made a mental note to look into that for the army. Reusable weapons were not a bad idea. Charlie was leaning on the wall on his side, his tomahawks held loosely in his hands. The four scouts were leaning on the cars, having amassed a pile of corpses in between them.

"All clear?" I asked, picking up my knife.

"All clear," came the response.

I waved at the archer on the rooftop. "My thanks!" I called.

"Anytime, mi'lord!" the man called back. He grinned like a loon and then dropped out of sight.

We burned our weapons free of the zombie gunk, and drove back to the camp. I had a few words for the scouts, and then we informed the rest of the camp about the fair. For a lot of people it was a welcome distraction, and a steady stream of cars and trucks headed south. Everyone was warned we were still in zombie country as Sarah reminded me when she found out how close of a fight I just had.

As the sun set, my mind turned north and to the other part of the army that was moving through cold country. It was late November, and they should be able to clear out that territory quickly. With luck, they would be able to make it to Denver at the right time. We had our own work to do, and since we were heading south, it was going to get worse for us before it got better.

Three days after we found the Faire, Sarah joined the scouting party that was headed south. We were still in open country, but we needed to get moving. The rest we had was what a lot of people needed to feel alive again, and with December somewhere ahead of us, we still had a lot of work to do and a lot of ground to cover if we were going to use the winter to full advantage.

TULSA, OK

"Okay. I am officially freaked out."

"Coming from you, that's actually frightening."

"I'm serious. There is just something wrong here."

"What was your first clue? The fact that there's supposed to be a few hundred thousand zombies here, and we've seen none of them? The fact that the ones we've seen have been, how shall I say it, shy? Or the fact that since it's been warmer than usual, there should be a lot of activity, but we've seen none?"

"I'm freaked out because Tucker wouldn't leave the back of the trailer. He took one sniff of the air, poofed out his tail, and ran."

"Now I'm freaked out."

"Would you two shut up already?" I said, trying to look around a corner. "I thought I heard something."

We'd cleared out Arkansas and then waited three weeks while another two thousand fighters went through Louisiana. That actually turned out to be an interesting run. Some smart gents on the north side of Mississippi River got it in their heads to open the dikes along the banks, and the resulting floods had pushed the dead in the city of New Orleans out to sea. What was left didn't take too much work, and the state was cleared without much incident. I'd heard the rumor of the floating cities out in the gulf where people had taken refuge on the oil platforms, but I didn't have much interest in bothering them.

Sarah and the boys had gone back to Starved Rock after we had celebrated an early Christmas. We had received word that Tommy's wife Angela and their child were not feeling well, so Sarah and Rebecca made the trip back with Janna and Kayla. They were going to meet us out in the plains again once winter was over. By that time I hoped to be on the other side of Texas, but who knew? We were maintaining our army by picking up recruits, and we were repopulating several cleared areas.

Right now I was in downtown Tulsa, and it was dead. We'd seen dozens of places like this, and the story was all the same.

Thousands of cars abandoned in the streets, bodies and skeletons all over the place. After you see a few hundred of these places, you start to read the details, and the story begins to unfold. The place where there are few cars but lots of bloodstains is typically a health center or hospital, ground zero for the rising of the dead. From there, you'll see the traffic start to pile up as people stopped to look at the disaster unfolding before them. You'll see lots of cars broken into, and in many cases the interiors will be black with blood and gore. The worst ones are the vehicles that have bloody car seats in them where children were helpless as dead hands reached to tear them apart. The carnage and destruction will spread out in a circular pattern from there, and inside homes you'll see blood and destruction starting from the bedrooms on out as sick loved ones turned on their families.

The piles of corpses and broken barricades will let you know where someone made a stand, where the zombies were fought off until the ammo ran out, the barricades were overrun, or the people managed to flee once they had no other option. Sometimes you'd see a couple of corpses with wounds that were definitely self-inflicted.

Farther out from the epicenter you'll find the occasional zombie drifting around. They've killed everything worth killing within a three-mile radius of when it all fell apart. Crowds will be even further, and then you'll have the drifting hordes that have nothing else to do but travel from town to town, finishing off anything that didn't die at first.

In a weird kind of irony, if everyone had just stayed home during the first two weeks of the sickness, it likely would have been contained. If the government had been honest and not tried to set up state centers, more would have survived.

Sometimes, though, the zombies didn't follow the regular patterns. Sometimes they just stayed in a certain location and did not wander off into the countryside. Sometimes they hit a barricade and turned around. That was what kept a lot of zombies inside cities.

I looked around the corner and checked the street. There was a line of rusting cars from here to the end of the block. Most of them had been abandoned, although some had been broken into.

From where I was, I could see most of them were not occupied, but there were a few I wasn't sure of.

I waited a minute while the wind stirred a bunch of papers and leaves. Nothing came out of the buildings to investigate the noise, so I ruled out the option of fresh zombies. The older ones had learned to ignore minor rustlings here and there, and we would find a lot of them inside, waiting to attack when something walked by. One of our groups used a dog to go to each doorway and bark. They caught a lot of lurking Z's that way.

I looked back at my yapping companions, and I figured I had good claim on canine help myself.

"I'm going to head down the left side; Tommy, you take the middle, and Duncan, you're on the right," I said.

"How come I always go on the right?" Duncan whined.

"Because I freaking *said* so!" I snapped. "Now go find some zombies before I send you to your room!" I said, smiling.

Tommy opened his mouth, but I cut him off.

"You looking for a time out, mister?" I said, pointing at his face.

Tommy dropped his head and stamped his feet as he made his way to the center of the street.

"You're ruining my life!" Tommy said, grinning as he pulled out his new melee weapon. The blacksmith at the Renaissance Faire had been busy, updating and improving some of our inventory for killing zombies. He still had his long handled axe, but now he had a new weapon that was a long wooden handle topped with three metal bands. Each band had four metal spikes pointing in the four directions. The spikes were staggered in a spiral, so no matter how it was swung, something was going to get pierced. Use against a living person, and that thing would cripple you wherever it struck

The blacksmith wanted to upgrade my pickaxe, but I was so used to it I just couldn't think to alter it. It wasn't broke, so I wasn't going to fix it.

Duncan had played with the swords, but he was still on the fence on how well they would work. I knew he would eventually get one just because it was different, but it would likely be later when he could practice first.

We walked down 6^(th) street, passing by shops and offices. Most of the buildings weren't too tall, likely because of the tornados that this city saw on a regular basis. There was a small park that was overgrown with grass and weeds to our right, but we still weren't seeing the enemy.

Tommy held up a hand. Duncan and I immediately stopped and brought up our weapons.

"Did you hear that?" Tommy asked.

"Hear what?" I asked back.

"Sounded like a zombie groan," he said.

I shook my head and looked over at Duncan. He shrugged and shook his head.

We kept working our way down the street and turned left down South Boston Avenue. The buildings got a little taller, and the view was much more narrow, but the tallest building was only about thirty stories high. There were a lot more dead people lying around and a lot more damage to buildings and storefronts. Several cars had been driven into stores, and their drivers were still in them.

Tommy stepped on a manhole cover and immediately there was some sort of noise. He looked over at me as if to say he told me so, when Duncan jumped in.

"Sounded like an echo to me," he said.

"What would you know about anything?" Tommy asked. "You're wrong ten times a day before breakfast, everyone knows that.

"You wish you were only that successful," Duncan retorted.

I raised a hand. "Question."

"Yes?" The two of them looked at me like innocent babes at Christmas.

"Do you think the zombies are in the buildings?"

"No, we'd have seen something by now," Duncan said, taking a quick look over his shoulder into the store.

"What about the countryside?" I asked.

"Same answer," said Tommy.

"Tell me what's left," I asked.

They thought for a minute. In the silence there was another groan, faint, like it was far away, but it seemed right next to us.

Tommy looked down. "You don't think…"

Duncan looked at me and I shrugged. "I've never been to Tulsa before. Do

they have a subway system?"

"Not that I know of. Sewers?" Duncan asked.

"Could be. Might be an opportunity here," I said. "If we could get to where the entrance is, bottle it up, we could just stand by and let them walk out single file to get killed," I said.

The groan underneath us was suddenly amplified by several more groans. We walked a little further on, stepping around a lot of debris, broken glass, and scattered bones. Some of the bones weren't human, and several were the bones of loyal dogs that tried to defend their masters.

"Where do you think the entrance is?" Tommy asked, tapping on a manhole cover as he passed it by.

Duncan shrugged. "Offhand, I'd say somewhere under that building up there," he said, pointing to a tall building about two blocks away.

The building looked like it had been built in the nineteen thirties, with a lot of decorative masonry and stonework. It was a good-sized building, about twenty-five stories tall, with a rich green roof. On the ground floor, there looked to have been a bank and a restaurant of some sort. There was also about a thousand zombies literally pouring out of the front entrance. They were moving slowly, thanks to the cold air of December, but they were moving with the same level of determination as a nice warm zombie in the middle of Georgia in August.

"Holy…" Tommy started, but never finished.

"This way!" I yelled, glancing over my shoulder to make sure the two men were behind me. We turned a corner and ran away from the sudden avalanche of dead people, wanting to make sure we put as much distance between us as we could. Four blocks later, we all put on the brakes as another building vomited ghouls in our direction.

"Dammit! We're running out of directions," Tommy said.

"Come on, this way!" Duncan said. He ran towards the horde, with us on his heels, and then quickly turned down an alleyway.

Tommy and I followed, chased by the groans and moans of the hordes spilling out of the ground like Hell had spat them back.

We turned left, then right, then another right, and finally skidded to a stop out into another street.

We had a second to turn around since the first horde had reached our first point of contact, and Duncan had unerringly led us right back to them.

"Nice orienteering, knucklehead," Tommy said as he ran past Duncan.

"How was I supposed to know they were going to be there already?" Duncan protested.

"We can argue later, let's just get the hell out of here," I said.

"How about up?" Tommy said. "We can lose them that way."

"For how long? They're out of their lair and know we're around here somewhere. They'll drift for weeks," Duncan said.

"Let's get inside and see if we can avoid them on the ground floor and then try to slip past. There has to be an end to them and we can get around them. If they're chasing us then it won't matter too much, "I said. I went to the nearest door and shrugged off my backpack. Pulling out my little crowbar, I went to work on the door.

The stupid thing was rusty and took a lot longer than it should have. Duncan was practically dancing, and Tommy was nervously glancing up and down the alley. I could hear the ghouls moaning somewhere behind me, and in the confines of downtown Tulsa, the tall buildings created an echoing effect that was somewhat distracting.

"Come on, John. How long are you going to play with that door?" Duncan asked.

"Any help would be nice," I replied, forgoing the quiet protocol and jamming my crowbar into the space between the door and the frame.

"How hard can it be?" Duncan asked, pulling out his own crowbar. He jammed the flat end into the same space and gave a huge pull that achieved exactly nothing.

I gave him a look. "Pretty dammed hard, I'd say, wouldn't you?"

"Hang on, pull your end again. Okay, I see what the problem is." Duncan placed his crowbar a little more strategically. "Pull your end a little more, and hold it...here!"

The door finally cracked open, and since Tommy was the one holding his rifle he ducked in first, leading with his weapon light. We closed the door behind us and tried to find something to block it with, but there wasn't anything nearby. We weren't going to be sticking around long, so we just kept moving.

"Where are we?" Duncan asked.

"No idea," I said. "It just seemed like a good place to get out of the street."

"I think I see a way to the main area," Tommy said. "Follow me."

Tommy wound his way through several offices and storerooms, staying on a path through the small maze. We passed a kitchen, a Laundromat, and a custodian closet. Finally, we stepped through an access door to a large, decorated foyer. It looked like a huge hotel but without the front desk. There was a café across the way, a men's clothing shop, a newsstand, and two very large escalators going up to the second and possibly third floors. Along the back wall was a large bank of elevators. Above each one was a listing of the floors that particular elevator once reached.

I looked over at the revolving doors and saw a familiar shape stumble by.

"We need to get out of here. If they think we're in here, that door isn't going to hold them," I said.

"Let's get upstairs," Duncan said.

Right as he said that there was a large crash, and a huge zombie fell through the doors. He struggled with the revolving door, and Duncan quickly stepped up and killed the beast. When he looked back, he shook his head.

"We're idiots. The skylight from up above may as well have been a sign to come and eat us. They can totally see us," Duncan said.

Another zombie crashed into the door, then another, and another. Behind those, there was a sea of monsters waiting to come in and devour us.

"You were saying something, Duncan?" Tommy asked.

"Just get moving."

We bolted for the escalators, taking two at a time. At the top we wedged a nearby table into one opening and put two chairs onto the other. It wouldn't hold for long, but if we could get a few tumbling down, it might buy us a few minutes.

Tommy broke through a door, and we found ourselves in the offices of some sort of legal agency. There were file cabinets as far as the eye could see, half a dozen conference rooms, and a large legal library on the far side. Behind us was a large bank of windows, but a quick look showed us that getting out that way would be less than helpful, since it was an atrium in the center of the building. It was then that we realized the entire building was built in a square, so anything that chased us around one floor, would just run us into their friends that were a little slower getting up the stairs.

"Street side windows, "I said, running around a bunch of desks and cabinets. Tommy and Duncan followed after they jammed the door to the office closed.

We reached the windows and looked down. There were about two or three thousand zombies down there on the street, most of them following the crowd as they stormed the building. Chances were pretty good there were a few hundred milling about in the lobby area, and in a few minutes, they would be upstairs trying to kill us.

"Thoughts?" Duncan asked.

"Have you got anything in your backpack that might help us?" Tommy asked.

"Nothing that wouldn't kill us as well," Duncan said thoughtfully.

"And you carry these things around with you," Tommy said. "Remind me not to get too close in the future."

"I have an idea," I said. "But it's going to take timing."

"Lay it out," Tommy said. "Anything besides blowing up."

A large crash at the door answered for me, and we looked at each other.

"Looks like time's up," Duncan said.

"Help me with the glass," I said. I took my pick out and cracked a small hole in the glass. I stuck the pick through and pulled back, cracking off a large piece that Duncan cleared away. I use the pick again and Tommy was able to pull out a substantial piece. Pretty soon we had the window cleared and were able to look down onto the street. The height was deceptive. It looked like the ground was closer than it was, and we would easily break an ankle or leg if we thought to jump now.

The zombies were still working their way inside, and fortunately none of them had seen us.

"Now what?" Duncan asked. Another crash on the door, and this time there was the sound of something breaking.

"Each of us need to push three desks to the center and get ready to get them out the window. I'll go first. You two come right behind me. We need to get these out as fast as possible. When the first one hits the street, the next two need to be right behind it," I said.

The two men instantly understood what I was talking about and hurried off to get the desks. I lined up my first one, then two more. Tommy put three out, and Duncan did the same. The desks slid pretty easily on the tile floor, my only concern was stopping myself from following it out the window.

There was another crash at the entrance and the distinctive sound of a door flying open and slamming into the wall. There was a general groan as the zombies caught our scent, and it was only a matter of time before we were out of room.

I got behind the first desk and raced towards the window. I shoved it out as far as I could, and dove to the side to keep from going out with it. I ran back as Tommy flew past me, launching another desk out onto the street. Duncan was next, and his went out with as much grace as the other two. I didn't waste time admiring the handiwork, I just ran for the next desk in line and shoved it out the window, with Tommy and Duncan right behind me. The last desk went out, and we didn't have time to admire our creation.

"Jump!" I said, pushing over several file cabinets to try and slow down the zombies who were looking for either legal advice or a tasty human treat. I wasn't in the mood to provide either.

I went over to the window to see Duncan and Tommy clamber down the small mountain of desks we had thrown out the window. The zombies who hadn't entered the building were making their way over to the mess, and I had better land correctly, or I was going to be on the receiving end of some very hungry ghouls.

I jumped down, sliding a bit on the surface of the top desk, but getting over to the correct side. I stepped down onto the next one, and my foot got caught in a drawer sending me headlong into the bottom desk. An intense pain flared in my leg as something sharp dug into my thigh.

"Dammit!" I yelled, falling to the ground. I held my leg and rocked back and forth, cursing the entire time. Duncan and Tommy raced over and tried to help me up.

"What happened? You okay?" Tommy asked as I jumped on one leg.

"Did you get bit?" Duncan asked, worried.

I grimaced and tried to walk, but my leg was not cooperating. Every time I tried to put weight on it I stumbled.

"No, I'm not bit. I think a corner of a desk jabbed me in my leg when I fell," I said, jumping forward.

"Well, that's good, but we'll all be a little bitten if we stick around here," Tommy said. To emphasize his point, several zombies were starting to fall out of the window, flop around the desks, and land messily on the ground behind us. Two of them were able to get up and started our way.

"Are you kidding me?" Duncan asked. He pulled his pistol and shot them both, the sounds echoing loudly in the confines of the high rises. The noise caused another round of groans, and this time the groans came from all around us.

"I guess not," Tommy said. "Come on, we have to get out of here while we can. Can you make it?"

I nodded, stumbling forward. My leg was feeling better, although I figured I was going to have a hell of a bruise in the morning.

We moved slowly away, keeping ahead of the zombies that were getting colder the more time they spent out of their tunnel.

That was a good thing, because I could still only move at a slow walk, and it was a limping one at that.

We moved up a street and around another, trying to put as much distance as we could between us and the horde. The cars in the street were good for slowing them down, and I made use of them by leaning the hoods and trunks as I passed by.

"Do we have any idea at all where we are?" I asked, stumbling a bit when my hand slipped. I looked at Duncan. "And before you say Tulsa, I'd suggest you think about it first."

Duncan grinned, and as he turned away he shook his head. I knew him better than he hoped I did.

Tommy looked at the skyline, then checked a small map he pulled out of his coat. Two minutes later he gave us the bad news.

"We actually ran in exactly the opposite direction that we needed to go, and we've got about two hours of daylight left," he said.

"Shit." I had nothing else to say. I didn't want to spend the night in a city with thousands of zombies roaming the streets only to have to run for it again in the morning.

"Well, things could be worse," Tommy said.

"How?" I asked.

"I dunno. Just something people say. How's the leg?"

"Slightly better. Where's Duncan?" I asked, looking around.

"Not sure. Wait, there he is. What's he doing?"

"I'll be damned. He's riding a bike," I said. I shook my head as Duncan rode up on what was clearly a kid's bike. It had a large rear tire, a long banana seat, and a long front fork for the little tire on the front. It was a pedal-powered chopper. If I had had a bike like this when I was a kid, Michelle Braxton in the fourth grade would surely have wanted to be my girlfriend.

Duncan hopped off the bike with a smile and ran back to the bike shop he had found tucked in between a bagel shop and a locksmith. He came out leading a small mountain bike and another kid bike. This one had large front and rear tires with a tall set of handlebars. It was probably one of the strangest bikes I had ever seen.

"Ready?" Tommy asked, as I settled onto the mountain bike. Duncan was not about to give up the chopper.

"Let's get the hell out of here," I said. "We have to get the containment crews in here fast before these guys spread all over the place."

"Oh, right! Wait a minute!" Duncan said. He turned his bike around and fiddled with his pack. He came out holding a handful of small boxes, and started putting them on top of random cars we had already passed. Behind him, a lone zombie turned the corner and groaned like there was no tomorrow. Duncan put a finishing touch on a box, left it on top of a car, and ran back to us, plopping himself down on his seat.

"That should work," he said pedaling away. Tommy and I had to work a little hard to catch up, and I needed to keep my leg from cramping.

"Don't you ever worry about one of those things blowing up in your pack?" Tommy asked.

"No, not really," Duncan replied.

"Color me unsurprised."

We rode through the city, circling wide to avoid the zombies that had come out to play. It took us an hour, but we finally reached the outskirts were the containment crews had been waiting for us. We got more than a few odd looks regarding our transportation, but that didn't matter a bit. I got off my bike and limped painfully over to the captain of the containment crew.

"There's several thousand zombies wandering around the downtown area," I said. As I spoke, there was the sound of several explosions, and the ground trembled slightly underneath our feet.

I looked at the captain again. "Maybe a few less, I'm not really sure," I said as if nothing had happened.

The captain, a former road crew foreman, grinned and pounded on his earthmover three times. The men climbed aboard their machines and fired them up. The ground trembled again, this time as the machines rolled past.

I limped my way into camp, following Duncan and Tommy as we made our way back to the trailers. I practically fell through the doorway and clawed my way into the bench seat by in the kitchen.

Charlie was sitting in a captain's chair reading a small book. He looked up as we sat at the table.

"How was the walk?" he asked.

"Busy," I said. "What are you reading?"

"Book about Oklahoma. Did you know Tulsa had secret tunnels under several buildings and hotels? They used them to transport illegal booze during the twenties."

I looked over at Duncan and Tommy.

"You don't say."

MONTANA MOUNTAINS

Darnell woke before dawn, listening to the silence that usually indicated snowfall in the mountains. He and his daughter had spent nearly a month in a small cabin at the campsite furthest south along the trail. They had been spending time at the campsites with the notion that if they stuck close to the trail, it would be the last place anyone would expect to find them, and after the first snows, no one would bother to come after them anymore. They would figure them to be dead or gone forever, which suited Darnell just fine.

Darnell went over to the wood stove and rubbed his hands together to get the circulation going. He took out his knife and shaved some splinters off a small stick, and after arranging the kindling to take a flame, struck a match.

The little fire wasn't warm yet, but just the promise of heat was enough to ward off the chill that had permeated the small cottage. At this particular campsite, there was a small house, a visitor center, and four cabins just like this one. Inside the visitor center there was little to offer, having just a counter, a reception area, a storeroom, and bathrooms. There was a soda machine, but it looked like it hadn't been restocked since before the Upheaval.

The house was another matter. It was a caretaker's home, and by the looks of things, the caretaker had gone out to town at exactly the wrong time and never came back. Darnell and his daughter thought it wasn't right to just take over the house, so they set themselves up in the farthest cabin from the road. They did relieve the house of all the supplies and edible foodstuffs, so they were decently stocked for the coming months. The caretaker had evidently been a hunter and fisherman, and Darnell used the rod and flies to catch at least one meal every couple of days. Alison wanted to be useful, so she took over the longbow they found and practiced her hand at it. The man had no guns except a replica flintlock, and that wasn't exactly useful against zombies. The big compound bow they found was too heavy for Alison to try, but Darnell was able to manage it.

The fire grew bigger, and Darnell fed it a couple of small sticks. There had been a large supply of firewood at the house, and the pair had liberated a great deal of it. Darnell spent a day cutting a third of that wood into kindling, which wasn't easy since he had to do it as quietly as possible. He didn't know who might be out there, living or otherwise, and he'd rather not be disturbed by anyone.

To that end, Darnell had taken several pine branches and tied them together above the chimney. The smoke that came out of the cabin was dissipated before it got up in the air, and helped hide them from anyone who might be trying to locate them by their smoke signature.

Alison came out of one of the bedrooms and rubbed her eyes.

"Morning, daddy."

"Morning, sweetheart. Feel like pancakes today?" Darnell asked.

"Only if you let me make them," Alison chided with a smile. "Yours come out like glue."

Darnell smiled. "True, but you aren't hungry for a very long time afterwards."

"I'll get the mixture and skillet."

"After breakfast, I think we should hunt the hills to the south. I think I saw some animal up there the other day," Darnell said, blowing a little on the fire and opening the draft vent a bit more.

"Okay. It would be nice to have some meat for a change. No offense, but fish is getting old," Alison said.

"Keeps us alive, at least until we get out of the mountains," Darnell said.

"You've said that, like, a hundred times."

"Always true, every time."

"Ugh. Wisdom. Save me, someone."

After breakfast the pair picked up the bows and quivers and headed out. They crossed the river using the access road and made their way up into the hills. The sun was breaking over the hills and lighting up the peaks and contrasting them sharply with the valleys. As they moved higher, Darnell smelled the air, trying to see if he could discern their wood smoke. It was there, but faint. Hopefully, further off it would be gone altogether.

"Daddy!" Alison whispered as she pointed to the edge of the trees.

Darnell looked and saw a decent-sized rabbit casually moving around the base of one of the trees, looking them over with no apparent concern. Darnell figured this rabbit must have had some form of human contact in the past, and was unconcerned as long as the two kept their distance.

"All right, this one is yours. Take your time and make your first shot count." Darnell kept an eye on the rabbit as Alison slowly drew an arrow and nocked it. She drew back the arrow to her cheek and sighted along the shaft, keeping an eye on the rabbit.

A second later, the rabbit was impaled, the arrow striking it just behind the head and exiting out its throat. The animal jumped once and then fell, its legs twitching purely by reflex.

"Nice shot!" Darnell exclaimed. It wasn't Alison's first kill, yet she was beaming. It had been a difficult shot, being about twenty yards on a target that was barely the size of a lemon. "Were you aiming for the head?"

Alison shrugged. "It seemed the easiest, and we don't lose any meat."

Darnell chuckled. "Oh, regular hunter now, are you? Well, then, you can skin it and clean it."

"Ewww! Daddy! No! That's gross!" Alison complained.

"Shh!" Darnell raised a hand. Something had moved in the woods, sliding in between the trees. He raised his bow and sighted at the man who came closer, stumbling up the hill. It was a zombie, and Darnell waited until it cleared the trees and then loosed the shaft, piercing the zombie in the eye and dropping it in the snow.

"Nice shot, yourself, Dad," Alison said quietly. She had her own bow up with an arrow ready to fly if her father had missed. That was the drill they had practiced. If they came in contact with the zombies, they were to cover each other's shot if they could. That was also why they had practiced their archery for the last three weeks, several hours each day. Darnell saw that arrows were better than bullets because they could be retrieved and used again, and in a pinch, he could make his own.

"That zombie is oddly dressed for a person who should have died in the April of the Upheaval," Darnell said, walking closer. He went over to the dead man and turned him over.

"I'll be damned," Darnell said, more to himself. "Lance Clearwater. You should have stayed home." Darnell quickly removed his arrow and wiped it off on one of the furs the man was wearing.

"Who is he?" Alison asked.

"One of Luke Blacktail's scouts. Supposed to only work with his brother." I guess we may be seeing another zombie before too long."

"Dad, was he looking for us?"

"Not sure."

"What are we going to do?"

Darnell shrugged. "We'll put him up a tree, and if his brother shows up, we'll deal with him, and put him up a tree as well."

The pair struggled but managed to get the dead man up into the crook of a tree. Darnell muttered his way through a half-forgotten prayer, and the father and daughter went back down the hill with their kill. On the way, another rabbit jumped from a bush, and Alison's bow twanged. The rabbit was hit mid-air and tumbled to the ground.

"Show off," Darnell teased his daughter.

A week later, the pair celebrated Christmas as best they could. Darnell presented Alison with a handmade quiver ringed with rabbit fur. Alison gave her father a necklace made from wooden beads she carved herself. Darnell put it on with all the pride of a father receiving a gift from a child who made it in school.

"I'll wear it always. Thank you," Darnell said.

"You're welcome. You know what I wish, though, don't you?" Alison asked.

"I do," Darnell said, his eyes getting a little damp. "I wish your mother was here, too."

The two went to bed after dinner, and the world was quiet and chill. The snow fell in a light blanket, and the temperature dropped below zero for the first time that winter. A cold wind blew from the north, and the promise of more snow swirled over the mountains.

Darnell woke up in the middle of the night wrapped in his blankets. He'd gotten used to the sounds of the quiet woods, so when a new sound appeared, it woke him instantly.

That's not a sound I have heard in a while. Darnell thought to himself. *I wonder where they are going.*

The noise became louder, and Darnell rose out of his bed to see a small car drive by. But it was not like any car he had seen before. It was a like a little station wagon but prepared for war. It was resting on oversized tires and shocks, while the windows were covered with metal blinds. A roof rack held two cargo containers and several gas cans. Darnell could make out one person driving, but there seemed to be another person reading in the back.

The car drove on through the snow, heading north. Pretty soon they would reach the upper pass and head towards the community Cole Hobbes built. Darnell doubted they would be welcome with open arms.

He turned back towards his bed, his concern over the car fading. It wasn't his problem, Alison was, and running out in the middle of the night to warn complete strangers was a good way to get killed.

The sound of the car faded away, to be replaced by a much louder, harsher noise. Darnell went back to the window and the next sight took his breath away. Dozens of cars and trucks rode past following the first car. The dozens became hundreds, and after a while Darnell stopped counting. He wasn't even aware of Alison standing next to him.

"Who are they, Dad?" Alison asked with a small voice, startling her father.

"Not sure, but that's a lot of people moving through the territory," Darnell said. "Wonder if they are that army the scouts were talking about?" Darnell asked, more to himself than to Alison.

They watched the procession move through the woods and up the road, eventually disappearing into the dark, the trees and mountains swallowing up the sound of their passing.

Darnell sent his daughter to bed, and went back to his own. He thought for a long while about what Cole might do about an army coming up his back door. *If they're half as competent as they look, Hobbes might not have much to say about it,* Darnell thought as he drifted back to an uneasy sleep.

MONTANA COMMUNITY

"So what do I do with you?" Cole Hobbes said, looking over the man before him. He wasn't impressed with what he saw before him, but it took a lot to impress Cole Hobbes.

Two days ago, word came to Cole that a large force had come through the mountains, following the old logging roads. Cole knew them well, he'd been over them himself when he first came to Montana. Over the course of the last two years, he had been through them several times and knew how treacherous they could be. What this fool before him thought about moving a force that large through the trails, Cole would never know. There was a fork in the trail, and one path took you to the mountain, the other took you to the canyon.

The small army of two thousand men and women had taken the wrong trail, got themselves stuck in the canyon, and now were trapped at the base of the mountain. They couldn't get out without Cole's help, and he wasn't inclined to offer any.

"You came to my mountain with the thought of putting us under your control, didn't you?" Cole said.

Tom Haggerty shook his head. "That's not why we're here. The Commander in Chief has ordered us to clear any zombies from the northern states that we find and leave the communities that have survived the Upheaval to themselves that want to be left alone. That is the extent of my orders, and that is what I aim to do."

Cole looked at Luke Blacktail who was standing nearby. "Did your scouts ever come back?" he asked.

Luke shook his head. "I figure they are not coming back. I don't have any idea what has happened to them."

Cole turned to Haggerty. "Did you kill them?"

"No! We've seen no one, living or dead since we entered the mountains!" Haggerty protested. He was livid, more angry with himself than the situation. It was his decision to take the south trail to try and get off the mountain, and he led them right into that box canyon. The noise of the passing vehicles caused an avalanche which closed the trail behind them with thousands of tons of rocks and snow.

"Perhaps." Cole was enjoying himself, like a bully always does when his prey is helpless. "Well, I ask you again. What do I do with you? If I give you shovels it will take you a year to dig out the mess you are in. If I bring you up, you'll run us out or take us over."

"No! We would not. We would take what we could, head south, and rejoin our army," Haggerty protested.

"And bring them back here, I am sure," Carson Hobbes said.

Cole looked at Blacktail. "Take him back to his people. They have enough supplies to last a while, and the river at the bottom will feed them if they know how to fish."

Hobbes looked at Haggerty. "Maybe you'll have luck when the snow melts. Probably around May these parts."

"You can't! There's two thousand people down there!" Tom argued.

Cole waved a dismissive hand. "Your problem. You brought it with you."

Tom knew when he was not going to win an argument with this man. He'd seen them before, and they were all the same. Community leaders who let the power of their position get the better of them. It always ended badly. He looked down and missed the look that passed between Hobbes and Blacktail

Haggerty allowed himself to be led back to the rope swing that had brought him up. He tried to think about what John and Charlie would do in a situation like this. John would probably have told the Cole son of a bitch to go fuck himself and promise him that he'd be back to make him wish he'd played his hand smarter. Charlie would have probably upended the table and beat them all with it.

He smiled to himself as he walked to the canyon edge. It was an amusing thought, but not practical. John always said put the most number of people first, and even if you're wrong, you can't be blamed.

They reached the edge, and Haggerty set himself in the swing. He stepped over the edge, with two men holding the rope.

Haggerty looked at Blacktail and shook his head. "I wish he had been more reasonable."

Blacktail waited until Tom was suspended over the canyon edge.

"He was." Luke slipped his knife out and with a slash, sent Tom hurtling to the canyon floor.

"No!" Haggerty watched the jagged rocks rush towards him, and his last thought was he hoped John would show up soon.

Luke Blacktail looked over the edge of the cliff and watched as the people below ran towards their fallen leader. Several faces looked up, and Luke stepped back as several bullets whistled past his head.

Probably should have disarmed them first, he thought. Oh well, we can negotiate for them later when they are hungry enough.

"Set a rope by the cliff, do not let anyone walk near it. No point in giving them a target to shoot at," Luke said to his lieutenant.

Blacktail walked back to the main hall, ignoring the questioning looks coming from the people who lived in town. He went back to the conference room and sat down.

"Is it done?" Cole asked.

"It is. They won't trust us ever again. Not until they have to," Luke said.

"Good," Cole said. "Now then. Listen to me. I want to talk about a few things, but I need to know if I can count on you for complete support."

Luke bristled. "I think I just proved you could."

"Easy. I just wanted to hear it from you," Hobbes said. "We'll let them stew for a while, and in a couple of days we'll see if they want to talk." Cole turned to his son. "Go talk to the builders. See what it would take to drop a section of the canyon wall. Just as a demonstration."

Carson smiled and left the conference on his errand. Cole turned back to Luke. "I think we may have an opportunity here," Cole said.

"Really?" Luke asked. "What kind of opportunity?"

"This army has just worked their way across the northern states. The area is wide open and mostly free of zombies," Cole said.

Luke thought about it. "So we can get off this mountain?"

"That's the thought. There are huge tracks of land right to the east of us, free of zombies, and ripe for the taking," Cole said. "I imagine every single person here could claim ten thousand acres without even running out of room."

Luke thought about it. "And what about the rest of the army that this one belonged to?"

Cole smiled. "I doubt we'll have any trouble from them. These mountains are a dangerous place."

Far below the canyon wall, a group of men and women met within the confines of a small box truck.

"What can we do? Outside of shooting anyone who shows their face, we're trapped." The speaker was a small man named Harris.

"The army is trapped, yes. But we all are not." This came from a woman named Alice Dorn who was named the leader after they buried Haggerty. She continued.

"Two of our fighters are experienced rock climbers. They will get through the avalanche that trapped us here and head south to find the Commander. Right now I figure he has to be somewhere around Kansas, maybe Nebraska. The good news is that he's closer than he was a month ago, and that works for us. I don't know what this asshole has planned for us in this canyon, but we will not just roll over.

"Stan, put your sharpshooters on notice. Rotate in teams, and keep a watch on the cliff. If anyone gets curious, kill them." Alice was mad as hell at losing Tom. She was a forty-eight year old mother who lost two of her three children to the zombies. The fight she had with the zombies was vengeance, and this Hobbes person was in her way.

"Benny, inventory the supplies, and I mean all of them. Carolyn, you get your two climbers ready. I want them ready to go tonight. We will have a service for Tom, and while everyone is distracted on the one side of the canyon, those two are up and out. If we can get word to John, then I know he'll get to us."

Everyone in the room agreed. Not everyone, but most people liked John Talon, and knew he was loyal to his friends and the people who took his orders. It was just a matter of getting word to him.

"Dismissed." Alice waited until everyone had left, then followed them outside. The river was loud and muffled the sounds of the camp. Alice shook her head. *We should have taken the damned other fork.*

NEBRASKA, WEST SIDE OF THE STATE

"Mother of God, it's cold."

"I know. The zombies practically shatter when you hit them."

"Useful that."

"Can you imagine the mess when all this melts?"

"Let's not be around to see that, hmm?"

"We missed Christmas, you know."

"I know. We'll celebrate when they come out to meet us in the spring."

"Here's to hoping we're still here in the spring."

"Amen, brother."

We were in Nebraska, slogging through the plains, killing everything we could find. A Norther with a bad attitude had come blowing in two days before, and the resulting chill literally took your breath away. The upside was that every zombie within a hundred miles was practically frozen stiff. I sent the army far and wide to go through every county and town and kill every single one they found. We cleared out hardware stores of hammers and sledges, since our edged weapons weren't very useful against corpsicles. Bullets worked, but if they couldn't chase you why would you waste a perfectly good bullet on them?

"What happened to Duncan and Tommy?"

"They went with a group over to the Air Force Base. Apparently there were some military survivors who had holed up there."

"Alive?"

"Nope. Enillo got in when they let in some civilians, and they were eaten from within."

"Same shit, different city."

Charlie walked over to a zombie that was stuck in the middle of a yard. Its eyes followed him as he came closer, and a hand slowly raised in an attempt to grab at him. Charlie brought his axe down quickly, splitting the Z's head like a melon. Charlie walked around the ghoul and raised his arm as he did so, leveraging his axe out of the dead man's skull. It was casual but effective.

I admired Charlie's choice of cold weather weapons since it took a second effort to pull the axe out of their heads. I was a bit lazier, choosing a log splitter. It was a long polymer handled thing, with a triangular hunk of steel on the end, kind of like a wedge of cheese. I had a choice of either an edge or a flat crushing surface. Either worked, and my preferred method was to raise it up and let gravity take over. Like I said, lazy.

We worked our way up the street, staying away from the houses and the businesses. There was another crew that was taking care of that, and they were ahead of us by six streets. The goal was to get through ten streets, end to end. Kill everything you find, and then you're done for the day. Usually it took only a day to get through a decent sized city. The dead basically just stood there and let us kill them.

Of course, we were freezing our asses off, and I was pretty sure I couldn't feel my left hand anymore, but we were almost done, anyway.

"Yours," Charlie said.

I walked over to a group of three zombies that were standing by a lamppost in the middle of one of those turnabouts that most drivers hated. The three watched me approach, and the one on the left actually managed a step in my direction. He must have been very hungry. His skin was grayish blue, and his eyes were freaky, being nearly all black. I mean, there wasn't any white at all. I was actually fascinated, staring at his eyes while he reached up for me.

"Umm, John? You hypnotized or something?" Charlie asked from the side of the road.

"Oh! Right!" I batted away the zombie's hand and brought the splitter down on the Z's skull. The other two slowly turned their heads, and I bashed both of them as well. The far zombie's head actually cracked into four pieces.

"What were you looking at?" Charlie asked.

"Hm? Oh! The first zombie didn't have any whites in his eyes. Pretty weird, actually," I said.

"Really?" Charlie walked over to the dead zombie and looked at its freaky eyes.

He came back a minute later. "That was weird. I think his eyes were bloodshot when he died, and the blood turned black as it spread out."

"That makes sense," I said.

"Shall we?" Charlie asked.

"By all means. How many roads do we have left? Two?" I asked.

"Umm, one actually."

"Nice. Should wrap this up by the end of the morning tomorrow," I said.

"Cool," Charlie said as he spotted another zombie. He walked over and slapped it in the forehead with the edge of the axe, knocking it off its feet and planting it in the snow. The zombie was an older woman who still had a couple of curlers in her hair. When Charlie hit her, two of the curlers went flying, and when she hit the ground, a few more flew up.

I was chuckling to myself and didn't hear the radio I had in my pocket. It took a few times before I realized my chest was calling my name.

I fumbled with my mitten before I could get the radio out of my pocket.

"Talon here."

"John, is that you?" Duncan was on the other end. Charlie heard the response, and I swear he sprained his eyeballs rolling them so hard.

I opted for sarcasm. It had been that kind of day.

"No, this is Jake, the other Talon," I said.

"Wait, what?" I actually think I heard Duncan working his head around that one.

"Jesus Christ! It's John! What do you want?" My hand was starting to freeze a little. If the wind chill was over twenty below I think I would have been surprised.

"Got a little problem. You might want to call in everyone for the day or get them inside somewhere," Duncan said.

I didn't argue or ask why. If Duncan thought it was a good idea to get everyone to safety, he had a very good reason to do so.

I switched the channel on the radio and made an all call to everyone within range.

"Attention! Attention! Attention! This is John Talon. All teams report to shelter or base. All teams, report to shelter or base until further notice. Talon out." I switched the channel back to Duncan.

"What's going on?" I asked. I realized we were about as far as we could be from base, and it was a long walk back to any warmth. My balaclava was starting to ice up, and my goggles were getting foggy.

"We were cleaning up the base, and found there were some kid zombies in here. They ran out of the base and got away through a hole in the fence," Duncan said.

"Wait a second. You said they ran? How could they have run? Why weren't they frozen?" I asked.

"When did I become an expert on creepy dead people?" Duncan said. "All I can tell you is what I saw."

I appreciated Duncan's sarcasm, so I got down to business. "All right. How many and what direction?"

"Sixteen, and they were headed north to northwest," Duncan said. "None of us got a shot off since they were too far away for pistol shots."

"So, essentially they're headed our way," I said.

"Sorry. Tommy and I are going to take to their trail as soon as we get our rifles," Duncan replied.

"Thanks for the heads up," I said. "Over."

I looked at Charlie. "You catch any of that?" I asked.

"Not really. Did he say something about rifles and a pistol shot?" Charlie asked.

I filled him in, and he was as surprised as I had been about the little ones.

"Son of a bitch! Does anything slow them down?" Charlie asked rhetorically.

"Just one thing that I know of. But we have a little problem," I said.

"Yeah, we don't have any long guns."

"And supposedly they're headed this way," I said.

"What's the play?" Charlie asked.

"I'm not much for hiding, and I'd rather sleep in my own bed tonight as opposed to some store or unfamiliar house," I said.

"Same here," Charlie said. "Let's make our way back, and with any luck we will catch up to another group. Safety in numbers and all that."

I nodded, and we headed south, going over one street and then down. I figured since we were already here we may as well finish the job.

We were three blocks down when I thought I saw something flitting between buildings off to my left. I stood still, thankful I had a line of trees behind me. I whistled softly to Charlie who froze as well. I waited, staring at the spot, and then I saw it again, this time it was a small dark shape that slipped along a wall, trying to stay in the shadows. I moved slowly, slipping off my mitten and putting my hand inside my coat. When the little zombie was about twenty yards away it stopped, sniffing the air. It was a boy, about eight or nine years old, with a crew cut and t-shirt. His eyes were ringed with black which emphasized the white parts. He kept his head to the small breeze, turning it this way and that, moving ever closer to where Charlie and I were.

There was a sound behind the zombie, and he whipped his head around, crouching like an animal at bay. Smelling the wind again, he moved back the way he came.

There was a blur and a crack, and suddenly the boy dropped to the ground, his skull having suddenly sprouted a tomahawk.

I watched as Charlie retrieved his hawk and did a mental calculation around how far he had been from zombie, and I reached a suitably impressive conclusion. That was at least a thirty yard throw, and he hit a target that was about the size of a cantaloupe.

Charlie jogged back, and at the far end of the street about six blocks away there was a cry as six more small zombies ran into view. They spread out to cover the street, and hurried towards us, their little feet churning the snow.

"Wish we had rifles right now," Charlie said.

"Got a handgun, but that's good for one if you're lucky and they hold still long enough," I said, watching the little horde get closer. They dodged around cars and trees, keeping us in sight as they got closer and closer.

"We going to run?" Charlie asked.

"Nope," I answered. "Don't feel like wasting my breath when it's this cold. "

"Let's restrict their access at least," Charlie said.

"Yeah, that'd be good. I like that box truck over there," I said, pointing to a roofing company truck parked in a driveway.

"Perfect." Charlie and I ran over to the truck and pulled on the back handle. The door was stuck fast and padlocked to boot.

"Not so perfect," Charlie said. "Another idea?"

"I like that porch over there," I said. It was on an older house that had a long porch covering the front. The porch had large brick arches going from one end to the other, and the owner thoughtfully had put wrought iron decorations that blocked the porch off. I thought it was a little ironic that the gate to the porch had a small sign n it that said 'Welcome.'

Charlie and I raced across the street just as the six little zombies rounded the corner. It was a race to see who would reach their objective first. Charlie flew across the yard and plowed into the gate, halting for a second to wrench the handle down and burst inside. I was right behind him and slid across the porch to crash into the front door. Charlie slammed the gate shut just as two of the little zombies slammed into it. They bounced off and then slammed into it again, reaching through the gaps in the iron. I took the log splitter and hammered the little girl on the left, trying to ignore the fact that she had large brown eyes like my son Jake's. Charlie cracked the skull of the other one, and we waited for the rest to arrive.

It didn't take long. The remaining four saw us and launched themselves at the gates. I had a small moment of panic when the gates on the far end didn't look like they were going to hold, but I only needed them to hold for a short amount of time, anyway.

I swung the splitter down, crushing one skull, then another. Charlie brought his axes out to play, and he had killed two of them without it being ridiculous.

A fifth one came out of nowhere, jumping at the bars and being repelled. She scrambled up, trying to squeeze through the bars, and Charlie killed her for good the next time she came within reach.

We sat back and caught our breaths, exhaling mists of vapor into the chill air.

"Do you think the Upheaval would have been different if the zombie kids weren't so fast and dangerous?" Charlie asked. "I mean if they moved as slow as the rest?"

"Good question. Probably not as bad," I said. "Parents could more easily control the ones that were slow moving, and we could have gotten a handle on it sooner."

"We killed eight total here." Charlie counted. "How many did Duncan say were loose?"

"Sixteen, so we've accounted for half," I said. "Want to keep moving?" I asked.

Charlie shrugged. "This is a nice little setup, but we can't stay here forever."

We stepped back out into the streets, trying to see where the rest of the kids were. The sun was nearly directly overhead, and everything was bright. Even the sky was a brighter shade of blue, although that just made it look colder, if that was possible.

I walked ahead, with Charlie about five yards behind me. We stayed in the middle of the street, not wanting to be near any corners that might have surprises for us. I carried my log splitter on my shoulder while scanning from side to side. I had no idea where an attack might come from, but we had to keep moving. It was a risk to be out in the open like this, but I didn't like just sitting around waiting for something to happen. If they were out there, they needed to be killed, plain and simple.

We walked three blocks without incident, and I was beginning to think we might have gotten ahead of the remaining ones. Charlie seemed to think so to since he walked with a little more noise than he had before.

That was when we heard it. It was a sound you never forgot, if you managed to live after hearing it for the first time. Little wheezing breaths close together. The sound carried over the chill air, adding to the chill I already felt in my skin.

They were out there, they knew where we were, and they were coming for us.

"Where do you want to be?" Charlie asked.

I looked around. "I'm good here." Cars to the front and back, can't attack that way.

"All right. You want to do the honors, or should I? Charlie asked.

"Go for it."

Charlie took his axe and started tapping on the side of a car. The noise was irritating and loud enough to keep the attention of any zombie in the area. He tapped for about two minutes, then I took over. I lay the flat part of my splitter into a car roof and just tapped it back and forth. I was able to get more rhythm out of my instrument than Charlie, a fact that was not lost on him.

"Nice. Do you take requests?"

"Crab."

"Frozen crab."

"That, too," I said.

They came for us from the side, two girls and a boy. They were dressed for summer, which made the situation even weirder. They broke cover from in between two houses, and they were a hell of a lot closer than I originally thought they were.

The boy came at me, and I swung the splitter at his head. The heavy bit took him above the eye and put him down without a whisper. I pulled my pickaxe to face any other threats when Charlie bellowed.

"John!"

I spun around and saw Charlie wrestling with one of the girls while the other was clawing at his back, trying to bite him and climb him at the same time.

"Shit!" I grabbed the girl by the arm she was using to climb Charlie, and her head whipped around. When she saw me she lunged for my face, but I got an elbow in her neck and kept that from happening. I lifted her up and threw her away, denting a small car fender with her body.

It didn't even slow her down. She popped up and lunged again, coming in low and fast. I kicked her in the face and flipped her backwards, spilling her onto her back in the snow. I wasn't going to waste time so I stepped in with my pick and planted the spike into her forehead. I tried to wrench it out, but it stuck, so I bent over to rip it out.

Just as I did, I felt something pass over my back and crash into the car next to me. A zombie boy scrambled to his feet and jumped at me. I grabbed him by the waist and stood up, bringing the Z over my head and slamming him to the hard ground on his. There was nasty crack and the boy's kicking legs were still. I pulled my pick and looked around, not seeing any other threats.

I turned to Charlie. "You okay?"

Charlie shook his head. "That was too damn close. If you hadn't been here, they'd have gotten me for sure."

"How'd they get to you?" I was a bit concerned at how rattled Charlie was.

"Came at me at the same time, and the older one actually ducked when I swung at her. Before I could get a backswing in, she was on me. The other one took advantage and jumped on me. I was trying to shrug one off while keeping the other one away. If I could have gotten one to the ground I would have held her there with my boot while I killed the other one," Charlie said. He held out a hand. "Thanks, man."

I shook it. "Hell, we stopped keeping score a long time ago. Gonna have to ask God when we see him."

Charlie grinned. "Well, let's hope you're not too disappointed in heaven."

"Won't be me that's disappointed, brother."

"Dream on. Let's get the hell out of here."

We kept our march through the city, keeping an eye out for anything that was low, fast, and deadly. I tried to keep the mood light, but I was worried about Charlie. He was shaken, and that didn't happen to Charlie James. I'll need to keep an eye on him. It would kill me to have to send him back, but if he gets too careful out here, someone is going to get killed.

Halfway through the city, Duncan and Tommy pulled up in a truck. I was extremely grateful for the ride, especially in a warm vehicle. I think I left my feet back in the city since I couldn't feel them anymore. Charlie and I just slumped in the back seat as Tommy drove us to the camp.

"How many zombie kids are left?" I asked Duncan.

"Well, we got four, so there's twelve still out there," Duncan said. "We tracked those four through the snow, but the others got away from us."

Charlie opened his eyes. "No they, didn't. John and I took care of the rest."

Duncan's eyes got wide. "All of them? Damn."

I nodded. "It was a close thing. We took out some on a porch, and the rest came at us in the street. Charlie had two on him at one point. He's lucky he didn't get bit."

Charlie held up a hand. "Actually, I think I did."

Tommy slammed on the brakes, causing the truck to slide about fifty feet. He spun around in his seat and glared at Charlie.

"If this is another joke like your family's graves in Missouri, it's not fucking funny." Tommy was livid.

Charlie shook his head. He pulled off his glove, and on the back of his hand was a small bite mark. Four of the teeth marks had just made dents, but the fifth one had broken the skin.

"Didn't start to feel it until now. But it kind of stings, now that you mention it," Charlie said, quietly.

We sat in silence for a moment. I had no words to say. Charlie was my brother, plain and simple. We had been through death, fire, and more zombies than I cared to count. There was a black pit in my stomach that was threatening to consume me. I felt sadness mixed in with rage and hate.

I tried to pull it together for a second.

"Get us back to camp," I croaked.

Tommy nodded, his eyes full of his own tears. Duncan couldn't take his eyes off Charlie, as if he was trying to make him better through sheer force of will.

"It'll be okay, John," Charlie said quietly. "It'll be okay."

I didn't say anything while we drove back to camp. I didn't have the words. What could I say? What was I going to say to Rebecca or Julia? I just silently shook my head all the way back to camp.

We pulled up to the trailer and Charlie stumbled getting out of the truck. Tommy caught him and steadied him. We got him inside, and Duncan fired up the heaters, sending welcome warmth throughout the trailer. When Sarah, Rebecca, and Janna had gone back to Starved Rock for the winter, the four of us had moved into one trailer for the trip. It was tight, but we didn't spend much time there anyway.

Charlie took his gear off, and Duncan took his axe and tomahawks outside for cleaning. He handled them almost reverently, like they were precious artifacts. Charlie frowned at him.

"Ain't dead yet, doofus," he said.

"Shut up," Duncan replied.

"How do you feel?" I asked.

"It's weird. I can feel a kind of heat working its way up my arm. My head feels a little fuzzy, but it's not that bad," Charlie said.

He took off his coat and vest and stumbled into the front bedroom. He lay down and closed his eyes, his breathing still regular.

I left him and went to sit down with Tommy and Duncan. Both of them were in shock and just sat there staring ahead.

"Don't lose hope yet," I said.

Duncan looked at me. "How can you say that? He's been bit! He's going to turn into a zombie. We're going to have to kill him! Can you pull the trigger on him? I'm not sure I can."

I shook my head. "We will do what we have to. If he turns into a zombie, we'll put him down, because that's what he would want. Could you leave him to walk around like that?"

Duncan looked down. "No. But Charlie's been like my older brother."

"I know. And if it comes to that, it will be the hardest thing I will ever have to do," I said.

Tommy looked at me. "You've said 'if' twice now. What do you know that we don't?"

I rummaged through my pack and pulled out a plastic bag. Inside the bag was an envelope. I took that out and handed it to Tommy. Tommy took the letter and opened it. As he read, his eyes got wide and he looked at me with renewed hope. He showed it to Duncan, who smiled.

"So there's a chance?" he said.

"A good chance, yes." I said. "Charlie might still turn, but there's a good chance he won't. We just have to keep an eye on him."

"What about you?" Tommy said. "The letter mentioned that you were partially immune as well."

"I asked the doc about that, and she said it was weird. Half of the samples she took were immune from the virus, the other half weren't. It was like it depended on which virus showed up to work that day," I said.

"But Charlie…?"

"Charlie's blood resisted the virus every time. But that was with older virus strains. I don't know if he's resistant to a newer strain," I said.

Duncan thought about it. "Maybe it's not newer. These kids were infected at the base, and they've been there since it started."

"Good point. Let's see what happens," I said.

We got up to stand vigil at Charlie's side. When we went into the room the change was minimal. Charlie was laying on his back, his hands at his sides. He was sweating, and I could almost sense the battle taking place in his body.

We waited in silence, and suddenly Charlie's body jerked. He turned onto his side and curled up into a fetal position. He suddenly straightened and began to tremble. The veins on his arms stuck out, and the one nearest his bite were deep purple.

I put my hand on my Glock, not sure I was going to be able to do what had to be done should the worst happen.

Tommy saw me move and put his own gun in his hand. I appreciated his caution. It likely would take more than one bullet to put the big man down.

Charlie let out a long breath and then lay still. His chest heaved for a moment and then slowed down to a more normal pattern. He opened his eyes, blinked a few times, then sat up. He brought a hand up to his head, and then he stood up.

I pointed my gun at his head.

"Charlie?" I asked quietly.

Charlie turned towards me. He eyes were unfocused, and he blinked several times. He took a step towards me and raised a hand. He tapped on the gun and smiled.

"Thanks for the thought, but I think I'm okay," he said. "God, I have a headache."

Tommy, Duncan, and I all slumped down, the pressure and adrenaline leaving us in a rush. I holstered my gun and wrapped up Charlie in a bear hug.

"Be more careful next time, brother," I said after I let him go, and he had a chance to hug the other two.

Charlie nodded. "That sucked. Not sure I ever want to do that again."

"You and me both," I said.

Outside, the wind picked up, and the northern wind battered our camp. It was a bitter, freezing wind, and it was as if it was warning us about things to come.

MONTANA, CAMPSITE

Darnell Tibbles walked the logging road, an arrow ready in his bow. He was becoming quite the mountain man, reading signs and tracking animals. He didn't do it for fun; it was a matter of survival at this point. The snows had come down in earnest, blocking passes and covering the trees in a white blanket. The lower areas were not as bad, but there was still a good foot of snow on the ground.

For Darnell's purposes, that was fine. It allowed him to track prey and move without too much noise. He'd found some small snares at the house by his cabin, but he didn't want to use them for fear of scaring game away. They had been here for a good while and were well suited to last the winter.

Darnell knew it wasn't going to last. As soon as the snow broke in spring they'd have to get moving south. Cole was not one to leave things alone, and he'd send more men out through the passes as soon as they were cleared.

The quiet of the morning, with the sound of the river acting as a kind of white noise, coupled with the beauty of the trees and mountains, made Darnell feel a pang of regret at the thought of moving on. But he was honest with himself and knew that his daughter was going to have to eventually find her own way, with new people, and that certainly wasn't going to happen up here in the wilds of Montana. He owed it to her to get her out to a new place, a new community, where she could have her own life, not one shackled to her father.

Darnell suddenly frowned. He hadn't seen his daughter all morning, and she had gone up the trail to see if she could spot one of the elks that they had seen a couple days past. It would be nice to eat something besides rabbits and fish with the occasional venison tossed in. He hoped she was okay.

Across the river he heard a small sound and looked to see a sparrow eyeballing him from one of the tree branches. He liked sparrows, they had an attitude about life he found amusing. Nothing seemed to bother them, and they fit in wherever they went.

Looking back up the trail, Darnell was reminded of the caravan that had gone through a week ago. The snow had completely covered their passing, and unless you had been here to see it, you never would have known.

Darnell walked further, passing by the campsite where they had spent their first night in this area. It was like a godsend, and Darnell was still amazed they had come as far as they had. If they hadn't found the road, they surely would have died out there in the wild.

A cold blast of wind hit him in the face, and Darnell grimaced at the slap that had come all the way from Canada. It was bitter cold and smelled like snow. He'd have to remember to lay in an extra supply of firewood this evening. That wind also reminded him that Alison was still out there, and his focus now became figuring out what happened to his daughter.

"Alison!" Darnell called out. "Alison!"

He waited for a moment, then heard a reply.

"Dad! Up here! Help!"

Darnell ran towards the sound of Alison's voice, his paternal instincts kicking into high gear as most fathers do when they hear their children in trouble. He fought his way through several large drifts and nearly lost his footing a few times, but he struggled on, calling out for his daughter.

"Where are you?" Tibbles yelled.

"Up here! Under Duck Tail rock!"

That helped. When they were scouting the area, Darnell made sure the two of them could reference where they were by landmarks. This particular one was a small rocky outcropping that looked like the rear end of a duck as it searched underwater for food.

Darnell reached the reference point and saw his daughter standing over a large bundle. He let out a sigh, and was about to scold his daughter for worrying him when she was perfectly capable of dragging her own kill back to the camp, when the bundle moved and an arm raised weakly.

"Holy shit!" Darnell exclaimed. The mountains echoed his statement in three places before it dissipated.

"I found him in the high pass just past Piano Rock," Alison said.

Darnell did some mental math. "What the hell were you doing that far north?"

Alison pouted. "I was tracking an elk, and he was better at going through snow than I was."

"No matter now." Darnell looked at the man. He was about twenty years old and was dressed for war. He had a knife, a handgun, and a small axe. He wasn't dressed for the cold, and there looked to be a hole in his coat. Darnell asked the man if he could walk, but the man had passed out.

"Well, I don't know who his is, and I know every face in the settlement. He must have come from that group we saw drive by a week ago," Darnell said.

"What do we do with him?" Alison said.

"Let's get him to the cabin next to ours, and we'll go from there. He may not make it, but we'll try," Darnell said. In truth, he didn't think the boy had much of a chance.

"Go down to the cabin and get a fire going. I'll bring him down as best I can," Darnell said, handing Alison his bow and quiver.

"How are you going to do that? I barely got him here, and he was walking most of the time." She asked.

"Leave that to me," Darnell said. "Now get going." He watched his daughter work her way down to the base of the mountain then turned back to the man on the ground. He spoke to the unconscious man.

"My friend, I get the feeling you are going to cause a lot of trouble," Darnell said. He went over to large pine tree and cut away three branches with his hatchet. Taking them back to Duck Tail, he rolled the unconscious man onto the branches. It wasn't the best travois he could make, but he was in a hurry. Grabbing the stick ends, he pulled the man down the hill and onto the road. Darnell kept to the track he and Alison had made, being easier than trying to make his own way through the snow again.

Darnell dragged the man up to the cabin next to his and Alison's, and he was pleased to see smoke rising out of the chimney.

"Alison! I'm here! Help me with this guy, would you?" Darnell called. Alison came out and together they lifted the man off the makeshift sled and brought him inside. Alison had cleared a path and lay some bedding down near the stove that sent waves of heat across the room.

"Good job, sweetheart. Do me a favor while I get this man's shirt off and start a pan of water heating. He may be wounded, and we'll need to see what we can do," Darnell said.

Alison left and Darnell began to work on getting the man's clothes off. He removed the coat and weapons, and was working on the shirt, when he noticed the man's eyes open.

They were cloudy and full of fever, and Darnell suddenly worried the man had been bitten by a zombie, but he relaxed when the man focused on Darnell's face.

"T-trapped. We're trapped in the c-canyon," the man said weakly.

"Who is trapped? Your group?" Darnell asked. "What canyon?" Darnell figured he knew, but he could be wrong.

"Killed our l-leader. Dropped him over the edge." The man snarled, and Darnell felt pity for the man who watched his commander die in such a fashion.

"Climbed out. They shot my partner. Shot me." The man lay back, and Darnell quickly checked him over. Sure enough, there was a hole in the man's back, right below his shoulder blade, leaking blood. How he had managed to get this far was a miracle by anyone's religion.

"Rest easy, friend, we'll do what we can," Darnell said.

"I'm done. Find Talon. T-tell him where we are." The man's voice was weaker, more strained.

Darnell held the man's hand. "Where is he?" he asked.

"South. Find Talon," the man repeated and then slumped as he let out a long, rasping breath. He didn't breathe in again.

Darnell shook his head. "You died well friend. Your commander would be proud of you."

Alison spoke from the doorway. "He's dead?"

Darnell nodded. "Sorry sweetheart. He was shot in the back. Must have filled his lung. No idea how he made it to Piano Rock."

"We have to find Talon, whoever he is," Alison said. "We have to! If Hobbes has those people trapped in the canyon and killed their leader, then he'll kill them all if he gets the chance. He'll do anything to protect his little kingdom!"

Darnell sat up straight. The word kingdom made it clear. Suddenly it made sense. The expanding fences, the consolidating of his power. Hobbes wasn't looking to just survive, he was looking to start his own kingdom and give out land to the people on his side. Darnell had been half joking when he said monarchy to Luke Blacktail. If the group this man had belonged to had cleared out the Dakotas, then there were literally states up for grabs. Once entrenched, Hobbes would be hard to get out.

"You're right. We have to. Let's get this man buried. While I'm digging, you start putting some packs together. We have to find this Talon person," Darnell said.

Darnell covered the man with the blanket and went outside to get a pick from the tool shed. The ground was hard and digging was going to be tough. A hundred things were racing through his mind, and none of it was good. He was going to leave his safe, comfortable life and head south in the winter, trying to find a man who might be ten states away.

Darnell shook his head. *Why couldn't things ever be easy?* he thought. A sparrow on a nearby branch peeped at him, and Darnell shook his head.

"All right. All right. It's not about me," Darnell said to the sparrow.

The sparrow looked at him and then flew off, shaking a bunch of snow off the branch. Darnell looked at the pile of snow and shook his head again.

We're going to need a truck, Darnell thought.

NEBRASKA, SOUTHWESTERN EDGE

We were three weeks into Nebraska and were getting ready to head south. The majority of the army was back in the area, and we were going to do a major push into Texas. The plan was to sweep around the eastern section, down through the southern, and then hit the western part. We'd cross back up into Colorado about the same time the army that was sweeping through the northern states would be heading south, and we all would meet in the middle of Colorado. By that time, the spring should be here and the zombies would be in thaw mode, and it would be a good time to head home and take care of business before the fall and the next part of the war.

For the record, January sucks in Nebraska. There is little to stop the wind and snow, and in some places we saw drifts that were fifteen to twenty feet deep. If there was a zombie under that he could just stay there until spring.

Charlie was doing fine, and for a while he was held in an even higher esteem than he already was. But after a while there came some grumbling, and a few openly said that he shouldn't be giving orders, he should just go do the job himself since he was immune.

That stopped when I sent two of the loudest voices back to the capitol. I had them driven by a trusted friend, and he said he would make sure they got there and dropped off without any ceremony. I didn't need crap like that.

I had spent the last two weeks recruiting, and I hoped it would be enough. The rumors of a massive horde had started again, and I said out loud that I hoped it was true and that we found it soon. In this weather we could kill a zombie with a tap from a ball peen hammer.

I was out by myself, checking out farmhouses and small towns. I'd cleared three farms and a subdivision so far, with only fifteen frozen zombies to show for it. I'd run into several live souls who were surprised as hell to meet me.

I had to make my way carefully around here as the snow was all over the place, and there hadn't been a plow for four years. A trio of houses was on the right, and I was hoping things would be the same. I pulled up to the first home and left the car in the road. I didn't plan on getting stuck in anyone's driveway and have to walk back to camp.

I trudged through the snow, making my way to the first house. It was a brick ranch-style home with a small shed out back. I knocked on the door first, since people who were still using their homes didn't really appreciate having the front door kicked in, especially during the winter. Duncan found that out the hard way.

Two more knocks, and I tried the handle. The door opened easily, and I stepped inside. It was nice to be out of the wind, but it was still cold in the house. Everything seemed normal, and nothing seemed out of place. The furniture was all where it was supposed to be, and the general impression I got was this place had just been abandoned. I checked the cabinets for anything of value and came away with nothing.

The next house was like the first one, quiet and calm. I did find a small store of cans which I took with me, and then it was on to the last house. This one was another ranch, although it looked like there might be something in this one. I took the usual precautions and then went inside.

This house was different. The furniture was tossed all over the place, and there were dark stains sprayed all over the walls. Strange little chunks were here and there, and I didn't need an explanation as to what those might be. I walked carefully through the house, seeing the small playpen, the clothes in the corner, and the pile of empty beer cans and garbage in the kitchen.

I walked with my Glock out, since it wasn't easy to swing a log splitter indoors. The first bedroom was obviously a child's with a crib and a small dresser. The crib was empty, and the dresser drawers were open. Clothing was on the floor and by the closet, telling me this was a quick exit.

I went further into the home and noticed blood trails on the floor. Whatever happened in the living room worked its way down the hall. A bloody handprint was by the doorknob, and I slowly pushed the door in with my gun.

Inside the bedroom, a man lay on his back, his hand extended up to the night table. He had been stabbed several times, and the murder weapon was still in his gut. His eyes stared at the ceiling, seeing nothing. He was dressed in grubby jeans and wearing a simple white tee shirt which was stained purple with blood.

The bedroom had been tossed as well, and I noticed a picture of a small family on the dresser. The man was there, smiling for the camera, with his baby girl and wife. The wife was barely smiling, and had her hair over her face. If I was a betting man, I'd say she had the remains of a shiner in the picture.

The scene was beginning to become clear. What I thought had been a zombie attack turned out to be a domestic murder. And if I was any judge, the woman killed her husband right when the world ended and there was no police to be found.

I went over to the side table and pulled out the drawer, curious as to what the man was trying to get to. Inside the drawer was a just a single cartridge for a .45 automatic.

I nodded to the dead man. "Looks like you got what you deserved, jackass, and you made sure your wife and child could defend themselves against the zombies. Good work."

I left the house, not wanting to disturb anything, and a small part of me hoped the mother and her baby got away to safety.

Back at the car, the radio was squawking at me.

"John, are you there? John, come in! This is Tommy. John, you need to get back to camp, now!"

I picked up the microphone. "John here, Tommy. What's going on?"

"John, you need to get back to camp. There's a man here who says he needs to see you right away," Tommy said.

"What's this about?" I asked, turning the car around and using my previously made tracks to get back to camp.

"Just get back here. He says he knows about our army in the north."

"What about them?"

"We've got some big trouble."

"Be right there." I had a sinking feeling I wasn't going to like what I was about to hear.

BASE CAMP

Darnell and his daughter Alison had walked over fifty miles before they found a vehicle that could take them south. Everyone they tried had either a dead battery or bad gas. Alison finally found a car that would start, and that was only because it had been stored in a garage with its battery taken out and its fuel drained. Darnell had to find gas and a battery, and that took all of two days before they were able to get moving.

If he'd had his choice, Darnell would never have chosen this vehicle. It was a 1969 Camaro, electric blue with twin racing stripes over the hood and rear. The rear wheel drive was awful for driving in the snow, and the thing barely got decent gas mileage to get them anywhere. It took longer to forage for gas than it did to drive a few hundred miles. After two weeks in the thing, Darnell was ready to ditch it and find something else.

But that was when he ran into the first few fighters from the army. They were a couple of nice kids carrying really big weapons, and they politely pointed him in the direction he needed to go once he explained he need to see a man named Talon. The two boys smiled at Alison, and she smiled shyly back. Darnell was happy to leave that behind.

Another few days of travel found him at the camp of the largest gathering of people he had seen since before the Upheaval. People came out of their trailers, campers, and buses to look at the hot rod moving through the camp. It was an orderly place, and it looked like they were getting ready to move on.

Darnell asked a man where he might find Talon, and the man pointed to a small trailer attached to a king cab pickup truck. A fuel truck was slowly moving through the camp refilling vehicles before the journey. Six semi trucks were parked on the road as well, and Darnell could see several men and women taking out supplies and putting in supplies.

Darnell parked the car and got out, waiting for his daughter to get out as well. Several older gentlemen gave Darnell a thumbs up on his vehicle. At least he hoped it was his vehicle and not his daughter.

Tibbles knocked on the door of the trailer, and it was opened by a medium-sized man with light brown hair. He had a kind face, yet his eyes were penetrating. Darnell doubted he could get away with lying to this man.

"Can I help you?"

"Yes, I'm Darnell Tibbles, and this is my daughter Alison. I need to see a man called Talon," Darnell said.

Tommy looked at the man and his daughter, his eyes missing nothing.

"I'm Tommy Carter. John's not here, but he should be back by the end of the day. You want me to send him a message?"

Darnell shrugged. "I need to talk to him. It's about the army you sent north."

"What about them?" Tommy asked.

"I think they are in serious trouble," Darnell said simply.

"Come on in. You can tell Charlie and me about it," Tommy said, holding the door open.

"Who's Charlie?" Alison asked, stepping into the trailer.

"I am," Charlie said. "Charlie James, Deputy Commander in Chief of the Army of the New United States. What can I do for you?"

Darnell and Alison were speechless for a moment. Charlie James was a huge man, with broad shoulders and thick arms and legs. He spoke in a kind voice, but the man radiated brute strength. Darnell had the odd thought that he had finally met the man who could take Cole Hobbes in a fight. Easily.

Darnell spoke for few minutes, relating what he knew about the settlement to the north, including the army that had passed by and the passing of the young man who had sent Darnell and his daughter south. Charlie's eyes narrowed, and he quietly asked a question.

"You said the man you rescued from the woods told you they dropped their commander into a canyon?" Charlie's voice was deep but quiet.

"Haggerty," Tommy said softly. He excused himself and went towards the front of the trailer. Darnell heard him talking to someone on the radio, and then he came back.

"John's on his way," Tommy said to Charlie.

Charlie nodded. "Good." He looked back at Darnell. "John will want to hear your story again."

Darnell shrugged. "That's fine." He looked at the two men again. *Hobbes will never know what he turned loose*, he thought.

The group made small talk while they waited for John. Darnell told the men all he knew about the community, about Hobbes and his men, and the flight that nearly killed the two of them. Charlie nodded appreciatively at how the pair survived.

"Have you thought about where you might go after this?" Charlie asked.

"Not really," Darnell said. "I wouldn't mind going somewhere with less snow."

"I hear that," Tommy said.

Charlie ignored him. "We could use a welder in the capitol, but you're free to go wherever you want. There's communities all over the place that would welcome you and your daughter. I would bypass Missouri, though."

"Thanks. We'll consider it."

There was the sound of a car pulling up outside, and Tommy looked out the window.

"John's here," he said.

Darnell didn't really know what to expect. He figured this John Talon would be some sort of ex-military, a short fireplug of a man, with a barrel chest and a perpetual cigar jammed in his teeth.

The man who entered the trailer was the complete opposite of Darnell's expectations. He was tall and broad shouldered, with powerful arms and hands. He moved like a large predator, deliberate and purposeful. If Charlie had impressed Darnell, John impressed him more. He looked like a man you would have to kill if you wanted to stop him.

John's eyes found Darnell and locked in, sliding into the chair on the other side of the table. He never broke eye contact as he spoke.

"I'm John Talon. You are?"

"Darnell Tibbles. This is my daughter Alison."

"Hi," Alison said in a small voice.

"Hello. Pleased to meet you both. Tommy says you have some information about some friends of ours?" John asked.

Darnell spent the next ten minutes going over what he had told Charlie and Tommy. Darnell watched John's face tighten when he told of the dying man's recounting of the death of their leader, and he could almost see the gears turning in John's head as he thought about what he had been told.

After Darnell finished, John nodded.

"You have my thanks, Mr. Tibbles. I owe you a debt. If you need anything, just say so. We'll provision you and set you up to go wherever you want. Is that Camaro yours?" John asked.

"Yes," Darnell answered. "Please trade me for something else. That thing is useless in snow unless you like sledding"

Tommy smiled. "We'll get you something better."

Charlie looked at John. "What's the play?"

John sat back and folded his arms. "Mr. Tibbles, I would ask that you find me the location of that community on a map." John turned to his comrades. "Tommy, get Duncan in here. You two will be leading the army south through Texas. Charlie and I are going to go north to get our people. They've already been captives three weeks, and I don't intend for them to stay that way much longer. "

Charlie and Tommy stood up and went about taking care of business. Charlie put a road map of Montana in front of Darnell and handed him a pen.

Darnell shook his head. "You're going up to get your people with just yourself and Mr. James there?"

John looked at Darnell for a long moment, and Darnell actually felt a little nervous.

"That's the plan. People who agreed to fight for the country and take my orders are up there, and I will not leave them to die. This Hobbes character killed three of my men. He will answer for it," John said. "Besides, I'll have an army with me on my way south."

Darnell wasn't much of a religious man, but right now he had the utmost faith that John Talon was going to handle this situation.

"It'll be freezing cold in those mountains," Darnell said.

"That's fine," John replied. "It will be warm by the time we get there."

"How's that?" Alison asked.

Charlie answered that question for John.

"Because we're bringing Hell with us."

CHECK OUT OTHER GREAT APOCALYPSE BOOKS

WHITE OUT
by Eric Dimbleby

An apocalyptic snowstorm sweeps the globe. Experts predict this freak storm will be "The New Ice Age." Electricity is gone, as are all forms of communication and road travel. As each member of a divided family tries to survive in their own way, they must deal with a snow-driven madness that has gripped the underlying evil in the hearts of men. In an epic struggle to get home and reunite, they will find that terror lies around every snow drift... and even in their very own backyard.

NIGHT PLAGUE
by Rowan Rook

Humankind will soon be extinct. A mysterious pandemic cut through two-thirds of the population in just four short years, and within another four, it will decimate everything – and everyone – left.

The last days are ticking by, relentless and ruthless, and the reclusive Mason Mild finds himself torn between a peaceful end and a brutal immortality. Between his hopeless, but comfortable days with his family, and something new...something violent and wild.

Have the fang marks above his heel dealt him an early demise or a second birth?

CHECK OUT OTHER GREAT APOCALYPSE BOOKS

THE DEAD FAMILIAR
by J.D. McKenna

In the twilight hours of a failing world, one man seeks to bring his loved ones to safety. Jack Hightower: Marine, bar-keep, and doomsday prepper. He knows of the coming calamity, and on the final night of an old world he seeks a new beginning.
This is the story of that night, the tale of how Jack and his survivor's colony in the north came to be.

DOMINION
by Doug Goodman

Dominion has been taken from man. Now, six friends must cross an apocalyptic wasteland dominated by a hell's menagerie of mega-fauna. Their middle-class suburban skills are no longer applicable to the world they live in. To find a safe haven in this world they will need to develop a new set of survival skills and fight the mutated denizens of the animal kingdom for every step of their terrifying journey.

CHECK OUT OTHER GREAT APOCALYPSE BOOKS

XY
by D.S. Lillico

An iron fortress protected by automated gun turrets is the only world Elsie has ever known.

When tragedy strikes, Elsie is forced to leave the sanctuary of her home and out into a brutal new world. A post-apocalyptic wasteland filled with savage mutants.

Hunted and alone Elsie stumbles into the care of a giant named Punch, but the world is now full of worse things than giants. Cannibals are starving, bandits are roaming and war is coming.

Elsie's arrival plunges the new-world further into darkness... and is there really something hidden inside of her?

SANCTUARY
by Ian Page

Deeta Nakshband, a Connecticut physician is attacked by a local surgeon while on duty in the hospital. Her friend, Janelle Jefferson, has similar experiences in Miami. Both of them become aware of an increasingly violent world as acts of isolated brutality escalate into civil unrest. They grapple with their paranoia as family members and coworkers become dangerously unpredictable. Worldwide, military units go rogue, war begins in Korea and cities implode as people slaughter each other in the streets. Martial law is declared in an attempt to maintain order. People are arrested, detainment camps are set up and interrogations end with tragic consequences as modern civilization crumbles. Deeta and Janelle band together with family friends and coworkers to save each other and find sanctuary.

www.ingramcontent.com/pod-product-compliance
Lightning Source LLC
Chambersburg PA
CBHW052002170626
46808CB00007B/2739